I0671379

Synz crawled on her arms bit by bit until she closed the distance to the door. With swollen fingers she reached up and twisted the handle. It came open. Synz sat up as the door swung wide.

"I came up earlier to see if you were okay. I was so worried until I heard him say how much he enjoyed what you were doing." Yandi said.

Yandi saw tears and immediately regretted her salty comment. She had tears in her eyes. Synz put her head down. Yandi reached out to for her.

"Don't cry for me, baby please." Synz said.

Synz En Detroit

By

© Inakat Publishing 2012

Detroit, MI

Synz En Detroit

All rights reserved.

No part of this book may be reproduced, scanned, or distributed in any printed or electronic form without permission. Please do not participate in or encourage the piracy of copyrighted materials in violation of the author's right. Purchase only authorized editions.

Cover Design By: © *Inakat Graphic Designs*

ISBN 978-0-9883533-0-5

LCCN: 2012920995

This book was printed in the United States of America

CHAPTER ONE – COME IN _____ 1

CHAPTER TWO - WELCOME INTO _____ 4

CHAPTER THREE - MIX UP _____ 7

CHAPTER FOUR - HELLO _____ 12

CHAPTER FIVE - TWISTED _____ 17

CHAPTER SIX - HE'S A FLIRT _____ 21

CHAPTER SEVEN - DAN _____ 24

CHAPTER EIGHT - THE SCALE _____ 30

CHAPTER NINE - HOOKED _____ 35

CHAPTER TEN- NO LOVE LOST _____ 38

CHAPTER ELEVEN - BACK STAGE PASS _____ 45

CHAPTER TWELVE- THE PRICE _____ 50

CHAPTER THIRTEEN - TWO OF HEARTS _____ 54

CHAPTER FOURTEEN- WHO IS THAT _____ 60

CHAPTER FIFTEEN - PAYLESS _____ 64

CHAPTER SIXTEEN -UNHINGED _____ 70

CHAPTER SEVENTEEN - 20 THOUSAND _____ 76

CHAPTER EIGHTEEN -HATEFUL   82

CHAPTER NINETEEN - FABLE   87

CHAPTER TWENTY - DIAMOND BASED PLAN   93

CHAPTER TWENTY ONE - HIT IT UP   96

CHAPTER TWENTY TWO - WHAT THE ...   100

CHAPTER TWENTY THREE - WASN'T ME   105

CHAPTER TWENTY FOUR - TASTE   109

CHAPTER TWENTY FIVE - TAKE THAT   114

CHAPTER TWENTY SIX - SHOCK   119

CHAPTER TWENTY SEVEN - SHOOK   123

CHAPTER TWENTY EIGHT -SHAKE   128

CHAPTER TWENTY NINE - STRING   131

CHAPTER THIRTY - THE SHINING   136

CHAPTER THIRTY ONE - INGRATE   140

CHAPTER THIRTY TWO - NOT YOURS   145

CHAPTER THIRTY THREE - MARCH   149

CHAPTER THIRTY FOUR - BAIT   154

CHAPTER THIRTY FIVE - WASP   **159**

CHAPTER THIRTY SIX - RUSH   **163**

CHAPTER THIRTY SEVEN - LOW   **167**

CHAPTER THIRTY EIGHT - CROWN HEIST   **173**

CHAPTER THIRTY NINE - ICED   **178**

CHAPTER FORTY - CLEAR PATH   **183**

CHAPTER FORTY ONE - FO' FIFTH   **188**

CHAPTER FORTY TWO - SIR PRIZE   **196**

Chapter One – Come in

The club had a Retro atmosphere. The bass pounded through the gray concrete floors vibrating into her bones from the heels of her boots. Synz's felt sexy. Hours before the show, she had been to the spa. Soft music played in background. Light chatter drifted through the air as the staff began to arrive with last details in preparations for the guests.

Her skin tone was dark cocoa and she stood five feet, three inches. Her striking figure sported perky breasts with a full moon shaped bottom that swung and swayed when she walked. Jet-black eyes and naturally full lips are what she considered her best facial features. Often she received compliments for features that never occurred to her, especially her toes.

As she walked in, she thought to her, *"Who are these newcomers?"*

Most of the people who visited were long time clients. Occasionally, someone brought a friend.

She stopped to smell the roses in the vase right inside the massive arched entrance. There were people standing along the wall awaiting instructions for the Spanking Room. A few people wore chaps and she giggled at the sight of them. Synz found the exposed butts funny because the odd shapes and sizes lumped together made quite a silly picture. It was almost show time and she need to get a move on.

After straightening her small frame, she strolled toward the crowd to address the loyal clients, returning visitors and first timers.

"Welcome to Club Black Fires. In just a moment, I will escort you to the auditorium. I am advising you to keep up with the group as there are many rooms and you could possibly get lost. I repeat, please stay with group.

Eight hours before the show, very important "Poo-nannie tickets" were auctioned. The winners will receive the luxury of detailed attention on a comfortable sofa. One person will also win another prize from me, in addition to the VIP treatment. Place your ticket stubs in the basket next to the couch.

Tonight's show is a demonstration of just a few of the fetishes that our group caters to.

Are there any questions?" Synz asked as she scanning the crowd.

She checked her nails and looked up to see curious faces looking back at her. Satisfied that no one had any questions, she headed toward the auditorium doors. The obedient group followed her into a room that contained a big semi-circled black leather couch. Each one put their stubs in a basket next to the couch for the raffle and sat down.

A man raced over to her and held out his ticket shyly. She looked at it and waved her hand, indicating to him to follow her to the sofa. She winked at him after he was seated and walked away with a coy smile. She looked back and saw his cheeks flush as he nervously rung his hands. It seemed he was new and curious about the lifestyle. The returning clients were relaxed, while he hung on to every word of her brief introduction. He might be the one she spent some time with after the show.

As soon as she saw the new guy, she thought about shoving a juice soaked thong down his throat. The new guy seemed as nervous as a puppy and unsure what to expect. His behavior made her believe he might enjoy some private time with Jamie as well. He rocked his legs and held his hand up to get Jamie's attention. Jamie went over to him and they spoke briefly.

Jamie was only a year into the lifestyle, yet he was excited to confront his inner wants. He was a cross-dresser that enjoyed pretending to be a bisexual female. Jamie had landed a high-powered job in the gaming industry several years prior. His day occupation required that he maintain a neat appearance and well-groomed persona. Having short hair and a smooth face worked out for wigs and make-up.

Chapter Two - Welcome Into

At the club, he had discovered a way to explore his expressive side. Jamie had begun to explore the woman within, thus letting her out to play. He once shared with Synz that the double life he led was a middle finger to society for rejecting him for being a cross dresser. As a teen, Jamie had dressed as the fabulous Patti Labelle for a Halloween party. His parents and peers made several insulting comments about his choice. Jamie had had worked hard to imitate the woman he saw as a pure Diva and had never felt more comfortable.

After an hour at the party had started, Jamie left early with his head held high while fighting back tears. Jamie believed he was beautiful woman inside. He was hurt when he realized that the people closest to him expected him to conform to what they saw. Even if he was a woman inside a man body, it was hidden beneath a male's body, and the world seemed to prefer that he kept it that way.

He became an angry adult because on the one hand he was constantly being told the key to happiness was truth. When he presented his true self, he was then told the key to happiness was to lie about him. Jamie finally decided that society was more uncomfortable with the rules they'd put in place than he was. However, in order to have any portion of acceptance he resolved to go along with the rules when he had to.

On this night, Jamie was dressed in a tan skirt set with black spike heels that showed off his firm legs. His makeup was just right, highlighting soulful eyes. Jamie had star potential. He could be gorgeous naturally as a man or woman. He had wavy hair, smoky eyes, thin lips, long lashes, and dark olive skin. He was so sexy. If she didn't know where his mouth had been, she might have kissed him. He gave oral sex in a way that made her want a penis.

Synz's understood from her own personal experiences that people often claimed to be whole-heartedly against anything other than a monogamous heterosexual lifestyle. Nevertheless, the same people spent billions of dollars every year at strip clubs, on porn and erotica in all forms, and on trade for sexual favors.

Synz and Jamie had bonded over the shared belief that Jane and Joe Average were more than likely mythical creatures than ordinary people. She'd been led to believe in the same ideals as Jamie had. Then she discovered through books that she'd read the same culture that insisted that it should rule people's sexuality had been indulged and benefitted since time began.

Every Wednesday night, since Jamie met Synz, he was a regular until a year ago. Synz liked his style and gave him a permanent position. Jamie job was to greet the guests as he made his way through the room and took drink orders.

The room they were in was a calm green color with lush tropical plants everywhere; there were fish tanks from the ceiling to floor on the far wall. It was outfitted with cameras, lights, and screens. The stage was hand built by a friend who was a carpenter and understood the specific needs of the establishment. Synz received a question from a patron. One of the security officers stopped the guest when he tried to approach her. He pouted when asked not to make a scene. She looked over at him.

"Excuse me Mistress, someone is asking to talk with you," Officer Whine said.

"I might answer one after I'm done," she said.

The Officer went back over to him and spoke with him. When Synz looked over their way, he had a huge grin. His smile turned to a pout when she walked up and placed a hand on his shoulder and escorted him back towards the couch. It was clear that the man wanted Synz's attention; he'd attempted to go around the woman that spoke to him. The client seemed to ignore the Officer's instruction, so Jamie walked over and took the man by the hand to seat him.

Synz's spent some time to talk to some of the clients prior to tonight. The backgrounds of the people who visited "Fires" varied. They searched for things that they had felt denied. Love, discipline, respect, authority, acceptance, attention, and the list went on. The grass always looked greener on the other side of the road.

Chapter Three - Mix up

The Mixologist came in through the side door and went straight into the Disc Jockey booth. When Synz's saw him enter the booth and put his headphones on, she headed to the stage. His arrival meant that show was due to start in a few moments. The women from the harem waited on pre-arranged cues the DJ to come to the stage. Synz gave her prop table a once over to make sure that all her equipment was there, before she walked over to the middle of the stage and took the microphone from the stand.

"Thank you for joining us tonight. As always, my heartfelt appreciation goes out to Jamie Stanley, our beautiful hostess. As well as the ever talented Mixologist and the entire Black Street Blend Crew. Lacy, our Detroit born winner of the Playa Pocket in the Midwest Contest, will be joining me onstage tonight," Synz announced.

A young woman appeared from behind the heavy curtains but stood still and waited for her next cue. Lacy is one of the women in the harem. Her fetish is oral sex. Her birth mother had a drug problem that consumed her. When she was six years old her mother gave her up for adoption. Her mother's plans were a better life for her but Lacy missed her. The adoption happened in the early eighties.

She spent the next three years to adjust to her new life. One day the couple came home with a young Asian woman. One week later, they sent Lacy off to boarding school. They told her that she was too old to be there and should finish her education with young women her age.

As soon as she after she'd arrived at the school, she fell into a depression and began to act out. She'd been sent home from school amid a scandal that involved one of the few men on campus.

Synz turned and looked at Lacy and put her hand up to her throat, which was Lacy's cue. Lacy stepped across the stage. She strolled out in link string bikini top, her bottom half was in a printed wrap around skirt and stilettos. Her breast bounced as she walked. The buttons popped and zippers opened in the audience as Synz gave her brief speech.

Lacy had twice pierced C cup breast with large nipples. She also had a healthy bottom and tiny waist with short, blonde hair. Her vaginal lips were puffy from a hot wax treatment that Synz's had given her just an hour before the show. Her body was toned and trimmed. A huge arrangement with rawhide straps attached to it for wrists and ankles stood upright on the stage. A robust male patron with thin silver hair waved Jamie over and whispered in his ear. Jamie had attended to the other clients on the couch near the man. . Jamie sat down next to him and put a seductively placed scarf across his lap and slid his hand under the scarf and began to massage the man's balls. Jamie whispered into the man's ear and Synz's noticed his expression changed and chuckled. The man removed the scarf from his lap and gave it back to him. Jamie and the man both continued to watch the performance without further conversation.

The start of the show officially began when she tapped her stiletto heel. Lacy removed her skirt and dropped onto the ground and assumed a doggy position with her head down. Synz walked over to a small prop table placed on the side of the stage. She returned with a whip, a feather, choker ball, white lace handkerchief and warmed oil.

Lacy reluctantly reached out to receive her safe handkerchief. Synz laid the other items on the floor then gathered her hair and tucked it into a loose bun.

Synz picked up Lacy's chain and led her to the wooden formation while Lacy followed on her hands and knees. When Synz was arrived to the spot on stage that she wanted to be in, she tugged at Lacy's chain with an upward motion. Lacy stood up then faced her mistress. Synz mouthed the word "eagle" to her and Lacy spread her hands to be tied to the posts with leather restraints. Once she was tied to the fixture and her back faced the crowd, Synz's poured heated coconut oil down the nape of her neck. Her hands worked feverishly to spread the oil until Lacy glistened like a shiny mint coin.

Synz walked behind the frame and attached small weighted clips to her nipples. The weights were handmade from simple clothespins, lug nuts and glitter yarn. Lacy moaned and drool began form in a glossy pool on her lips.

With delicate fingers, Synz's twisted the clips and watched her stiffen up defiantly. Her face held a look of fiery lust while Lacy pushed her body towards her. Synz's leaned in close as if to kiss her. She held her gaze as she rotated her hand, Synz directed the clip until Lacy's eyes watered and she dropped her head. Synz's wiped Lacy's face with her fingers, cupped her chin and raised her head back up before she took center stage again.

"Tonight you will get a glance of an unusual sexual play," she said to the crowd.

"Everything in here is unusual," Jamie yelled out.

The guests laughed in amusement at his quick wit.

Chapter Four - Hello

"Interrupt me again and you will be in the stockade for the rest of the show and someone else will take over your duties, are we clear?" Synz said.

"Yes Mistress, clear."

"Good."

Synz swaggered back across the stage seductively while let her behind jiggle like jelled fruit as she went. She picked up the whip from the ground. Synz felt a rush of excitement and closed in behind Lacy and sadistically swatted her lower back and ass with the whip. Burgundy streak marks popped up almost instantaneously. The bruises stood out boldly on her creamy skin and Lacy whimpered.

"Thank you Mistress, May I please have another?" Lacy mumbled.

"What did you say?" Synz asked.

"Unnngh."

The audience heard the whip crack as the leather stripes cut through the air when Synz's swung. It landed a direct hit on Lacy's bottom.

"Mmmmmm," Lacy groaned.

Synz's began to spank her harder. After about thirty lashes she felt she had had enough. Lacy's entire butt and thighs was covered in welts. Synz leaned over and opened Lacy's cheeks and slapped her gently on her ass hole a few times. All the while delicately, Synz ran her tongue over her shiny lips and savored the moment. Everyone in the room watched as her tiny open hole tensed.

Synz's bent down and picked up the feather and brushed it over the bruises on her bottom. Lacy purred with the change of sensations. Synz poured more oil into the crack of her ass and pushed the flog handle of the whip into her small anal slot. Lacy tried to twist away but couldn't move far. Synz's slid the knob between her greased lips and put it to Lacy's nose. Lacy inhaled it deeply while Synz's unsnapped the ball to remove it from her mouth.

"Please Mistress; I'll do whatever you want," Lacy said.

"Of course you will dear. Did you think that being a slave was some choice assignment in life?" Synz told her pointedly.

"No Mistress."

Synz scanned the audience and spotted a large muscular black man and motioned for him to come up. He sprinted to join them onstage while she released Lacy from her bonds and grabbed her chain. The man stood ready to help. Lacy rubbed her wrists tenderly but kept her head down. Synz cupped Lacy's chin firmly and once again pulled her head up.

Synz took a finger and put it between her own lips. Lacy nodded and unzipped his pants to unleash a solid thick twelve inches of courage. Synz's passed her a condom. She ripped the package open with her teeth and put the rubber in her mouth. Lacy knelt on her haunches and she waited for further instructions.

"Now, show them why you are here." She said.

She waved her hand and pointed at the crowd. Lacy went to work on his sac and as she stroked the shaft gently with her hand. The man formed an oval with his mouth. Nervously he scanned the crowd to look to see if his female companion watched. He spotted her in the crowd crossed her legs and sat on the edge of her seat. Lacy had rolled the condom over his already erect shaft with her hot mouth.

Lacy wet his sac thoroughly with her tongue before she finally turned around and pulled him sideways into her mouth with a loud wet slurp. He reached out to steady himself by grabbed Synz's arm and she snatched away. Lacy's sensual soft lips and excellent oral skills almost made him collapse.

He spread his legs to balance himself while he gripped the back of Lacy's head. He pumped into her lips. Lacy encouraged him and clutched his hips on both sides firmly. He grabbed the bottom of his hardness. His lips hung open as he lowered his head to look down at her.

"Are you serious? I want to hear him moan. And what are you on? Work her mouth deep and twist those weights." Synz's said.

Synz moved in and pinched her nose to cut off her air supply for a few seconds. The man looked up at Synz with a raised brow; it had caused him to appear to be slightly puzzled at Synz's actions. He began to grab and pull on Lacy's massive jugs. Lacy coughed when Synz's let go of her nostrils. A flood of saliva spewed out. The volunteer paused before he greeted the end of her spasms with a mouth full of shaft that went deep into her throat. The excessive slobber had caused her mouth to be extra wet, which allowed him to slide deeper much more easily.

"Ohhhhh", he said.

It was a gruesome sight for Synz's to watch her take on the challenge to pleasure a penis the size of a small baseball bat. Synz had seen many shafts but his was extraordinarily long and thick. The man reached down and wrapped her hair around his hand. The stranger rocked into her hot mouth rhythmically. Synz unbuttoned his shirt for a better view of his chest. The scene replayed live from a feed on a projection screen that hung from the wall. A video camera sat on a tripod trained on the center of the stage. She looked at the screen and suddenly felt nauseous. The room swirled and before she could speak another word she fell.

"Oh my goodness, not now." She thought.

The floor came up fast and she blacked out for the fifth time in three months. The last time this happened, she recalled a Good Samaritan shined a light in her face to wake her. She was dressed in a three-piece business suit and heels. Her briefcase, cell phone and purse lay undisturbed in the grass next to her. The cool wet wind gently patted her cheeks as her eyes adjusted to the dusky light. A portion of the rail that guarded the sparkly water of the Detroit River came into her view.

The man offered to call an ambulance for her. She declined. He looked her over and helped her up to go on about her way. Synz's couldn't remember how she'd come to be on Belle Isle.

Chapter Five - Twisted

Lunacy showed up in Sinclair's life shortly before her mother, January passed away. She was a stunning five foot three inch tall, woman. She migrated to Detroit in the midst of the riots and attempted to flee from the heights of the Southern Massacre. In 1964, she was just a tender teenager, which witnessed the brutal beatings of African-Americans from the Student Non-Violent Coordinating Committee. The group had visited her hometown of Meridian, Mississippi to help Blacks register to vote. Shortly after she'd expressed interest in their cause, January suffered a violent and malicious attack. She was on the way home from school when three adult men spotted her and released dogs on her. January barely escaped alive. Her arms, legs and torso bore permanent scars from the violence. That same year, Dr. M.L. King had won the Nobel Peace Prize. January's intention was to leave behind the hurt and anguish and start a new life.

January feared being unloved, because she was an orphan. She cared for others as her way of to give back a part of herself to the community. She felt that since others had stepped up in her time of need as a child, that she was indebted to do the same for someone else. She was attractive and cared for others, which made her all the more lovable. Jan was beautiful inside. A mother's love was a touch that she believed every child should feel.

Since January hadn't told Synz exactly what had caused her mother's departure, she grew up and questioned what would bring a mother to leave her child. Whatever the reasons, she had decided that she would not continue the cycle, but rather become an open advocate against what she assumed was an unwanted pregnancy. January was never shy about things of a sexual nature. She warned younger women against the easy swayed of compliments and the possible outcomes.

"You hear me clearly when I tell you; a hard penis doesn't have a conscious. He will tell you anything to get in your panties. Where I come from we call them B-boys, if you find yourself attracted to that kind You can play with him but don't give him nothing but a hard time. He might be quick to offer you a good time but those good times now can lead to babies you can't care for later. Children deserve parents that want them and to take care of them. The choice to do have sex or wait is entirely up to you. Just know that, sweet-talking don't always end in a sweet fairy-tale of happily ever after.

At some point, a real man is going come around trying to court you. You'll know he's real by the way he carries himself. Watch how he treats his mother and the women around him. If he mistreated the first women in his life, his mother, sisters, and grandmothers and so on, then that's probably how he'll treat you. Watch the people you call your friends. Try to use your head as a guide and your heart as a scale because this world can be cruel at times, but to have a good friend you have to be one." January warned them

Many years later share would tell Sinclair, that he'd met her mother on the first evening she rolled into the city. He worked at Penn Central Station in downtown Detroit at night as well as worked construction in the day. Markus had known from the first day he first saw her, that January was some extraordinary kind of special.

Markus had also shared with Synclaire that he'd felt her mother before he ever-laid eyes on January. When she stepped into the lobby of the place, they were drawn to each other almost instantly. They fell in love in that moment. He straightened his shirt and walked over to her.

"You are the most beautiful woman I have ever seen. Your husband must be worried sick," he said.

"Who me? I'm not married." she replied.

Markus reached down and grabbed her bags and they took the long walk to find a taxi for her while he made his case. He'd always been a take charge type of guy. He stood at five feet nine inches and two hundred and forty pounds of all muscle, with thick black wavy hair that he kept well-groomed. He had a light-complexion and sensuous with moves like a cat. His way with the women had an undeniable charm.

January settled in with her family that lived in Detroit and began school. A month after she arrived she had found a part-time job at Milo's Restaurant as a counter girl. She served hamburgers to the locals. January saved as much money as she could. In her spare time she took Foster Parent classes.

His construction job often took him away from the city, and sometimes the state. January had taken in two children while he was gone. He seemed upset at first, but his desire to be the man in her life was strong. Markus wanted a family with January, but realized that his absence meant she was alone. Because of he was the person that operated the bulldozer; he was the first person on a build- site and usually the last to get home.

It took little time to convince Markus, the children were better off with her than in foster care. January had a way with people, especially kids. Once she took them into her heart, they would always know what loved looked like. She cared for the children as if she had given birth to them. Markus was happy with whatever made January smile.

Chapter Six - He's a Flirt

These children were the first of many children she would care for. January's spirit was that of a dedicated caregiver. She often fed neighborhood children that she suspected could use extra love and attention. Six months after her arrival in Detroit, January had established herself in a small three-bedroom home. The house was always busy with the bustle of children she'd taught arts and crafts, to cook, and garner a love for music with her.

The young couple had kept in touch over the phone, whenever Markus was away. When he came back to the city, the two usually made plans to go out. One weekend, January had planned an overnight event for the kids at her aunt's house. When he arrived to the door to pick her up, she opened the door Markus was taken back. She had on a sexy knit skirt set and high heels. He stepped forward and wrapped his arms around her waist. A few seconds later the front door closed as they went inside instead.

By 1967 a riot had erupted in the city of Detroit. The state had now been deeply affected and was in a charged mood. People caught in the middle cried out for peace and fairness. One day the citizens tired of begging. The clash that erupted in Detroit as well as other parts of the United States had to do with money, power and respect. After years of unequal distribution of wealth, some decided the class system didn't work. The issues that January had hoped to leave behind were once again at her door.

Markus and January had seen each other regularly for nearly four years. She woke up one morning nauseated. It continued for the next few days then suddenly stopped. Shortly after, January began to experience low-back pain that also went away. She then began to feel tired and hungry more often than normal for her. When she told Markus about it, he asked her to wait until his return and they would to go the doctor together. Once they had made it to the doctor, she was asked to give urine and blood samples and she did. After what seemed like an eternity, the physician finally came in to speak with them. He told them that he ordered a pregnancy test. When the doctor informed them the results were positive, Markus could barely contain his excitement.

January wrung her hands nervously and visibly shuddered. When Markus noticed she wasn't happy and didn't smile, he lifted her chin and looked into her eyes.

"What's wrong?"

"I hadn't planned on us having any children of our own yet."

He stuck his hand into his pocket and produced a diamond ring.

"But I wanted to ask if you will you marry me? We already have a family. That's my baby so you might as well marry me."

"Marry you?"

"Yes, what did you think I was about to say?"

"I don't know. I hadn't thought about marriage or babies of our own."

"Well, you're carrying my child and I'd like it very much if you would be my wife. I was going to ask you anyway. We have been seeing each other for a while. What do you say? January will you marry me?"

"Yes"

He leaned down and kissed her softly on the lips. She took the ring and put it on. He leaned on to kiss her again. The doctor cleared his throat to get their attention. The physician reached out to shake Markus's hand.

"Congratulations to the both of you. Here's a prescription for prenatal vitamins. Take one every day, get plenty of rest, and exercise. I want you to stop at the desk and pick up an appointment card for your next visit," the doctor said.

Six weeks later, Markus and January were married. Because of the pregnancy, January and Markus wanted to keep things quiet and simple. The women in January's family heard the news and insisted on some type of a celebration. Januarys' aunties and girlfriends had organized a reception the next weekend.

After the wedding, the newlyweds sat down with their two daughters and told them about the baby. The girls were delighted. They squealed with laughter and rushed to rub January's belly. The subsequent year in April of 1969, January and Markus welcome a beautiful, healthy baby boy into their family.

It was almost five years later when Sinclair was born. January and Markus family would grow to include four daughters and one son. The children grew up and understood that their parents had high hopes for each of them. Neither parent could predict the path Synz would take as an adult. Twenty five years later, in a hotel lobby, it would become clear that the path that Synz had chosen was quite different than what they'd hoped for.

Chapter Seven - Dan

Dan was considered attractive by most women. However, he lacked the social skills to keep them. They found him a little out of the ordinary. He was at a lost for what to do, so he kept to him whenever he was in the company of the opposite sex.

He had sun kissed-bronze skin and dark blue eyes. Dan's thick, course hair was golden brown. At five feet and eleven inches tall, Dan weighed a sturdy two-hundred and twenty pounds. His neatly trimmed sideburns connected with his beard. Dan had keen Egyptian-like facial feature with a small pointed nose and high check-bones. His thick brows and pencil thin mustache made him appear sophisticated. His unusual combination of features for a black man earned him attention from women on a daily basis. Since he'd turned sixteen years old, females had thrown themselves at him. Dan had managed to avoid intimacy with a female until he was seventeen.

His first encounter with a female was a twisted affair. She was a neighborhood parent with a thing for much younger men. The woman had bought him expensive shoes and clothes to impress him. She allowed him to come to her house, to do what his mother wouldn't tolerate such as, to smoke and drink alcohol. It wasn't long before she took him to bed.

As a prepubescent child he wasn't outgoing. He didn't smile or play with other kids. His eyes were pools of fire in a chubby face. Later he grew into a handsome man with solid, rugged features. Dan was irresistible attractively.

Many years later, others who had met him would recall the small facts that helped shape him. Few people ever remembered him to have shown signs of fear and very little made him nervous. The sight of blood and guts neither excited nor disgusted him. His first grade teacher, Mrs. Novell, would be the first to realize something was astray. He remained curiously calm through events that would send most children his age into a panicked snot-filled frenzy.

A classmate's home had burned. Mrs. Novell gathered the children and gently explained what happened. A few of the children began to cry. Mrs. Novell squatted down and hugged them. As she comforted them, she felt a small finger tap her shoulder. Mrs. Novell instinctively reached out to hug the little person. It was Dan. He asked if he could begin his work.

Mrs. Novell agreed and told the students that she had a special assignment for them. The teacher told the children that they would all get to express their loss with a card and pictures for the family. She passed out materials for them to make their own little piece of a collage. She eyed Dan suspiciously when he took his items and sat in the child assigned chair, that his home. A few moments later she began to walk around the room to give encouragement and comments to her students. When she saw what Dan had drawn, she almost fainted.

Dan had drawn an elaborate multi-leveled house. The windows were busted and the faces of the people seemed to be in fear with their mouths opened. The roof of the house was ablaze. The details surprised her for a small child to have drawn.

Mrs. Novell had earned a bachelor's degree in Child Psychology. She'd studied many disorders that affected children. The very nature of the image caused her refer him to the school social worker. His mother was called to the school and the social worker showed the picture to her. Dan's mother argued that he was only a small child that didn't understand. She refused therapy for him. Dan's mother knew in her heart that she had a disturbed child on her hands.

At the tender age of six, Dan's mother had built a wall of denial about her child's behavior. He learned quickly that she would protect him. His mother's refusal to accept that there might be a problem with Dan, had given his dark personality a shelter to grow in. By Dan's eighteenth birthday, his mother had made sure he was enlisted in the military.

In the military, Dan excelled. Nevertheless, Dan decided not to re-enlist for a second stint. Instead, at the tender age of twenty, Dan opened a Catering Service. His mother wanted him to come home to stay with her. Dan politely turned her down. He informed her that he all set to move into an apartment on the farthest end of town.

By the age of thirty-one Dan had proven his was worth a financial wizard and insightful businessman. He traveled frequently. Although Dan was clean-cut, charming and well-spoken, he was single. Dan's thirty-second birthday fast approached and he decided to take a trip to Detroit to celebrate it quietly. He checked into the Ponchatrain Hotel.

When he arrived, he didn't want to go out to eat, but the prospect to sit in a hotel room alone had no appeal to him. Dan wanted to hear laughter and at least watch the people interact. He often found that if he studied the way cultures behaved, it made it easier for him to blend into a place unnoticed.

An hour after his arrival, Dan left the hotel and began to walk down Jefferson. When he reached Cobo Hall, he walked up Washington Boulevard until he reached Michigan Avenue. He had remembered to follow the wall that surrounded the Renaissance Center, until he saw where it sloped in solid ground. Dan searched for Sara Scales Restaurant. He'd come to the city several times a year and it was one of the few places that he knew.

The air blew a mild breeze as he strolled to the Arcade. The smell of grilled chicken wafted through the night. People crowded the sidewalks and worked their way up and busy downtown streets. As he approached his destination he noticed a petite woman, as she slid from a cab, in front of a Taco Bell across the street.

He gasped and stopped in his steps midstride. A passerby bumped into him and Dan muttered a quick apology, which snapped him back to reality. Suddenly, the woman had disappeared into a tall office building next to the restaurant. He couldn't put his finger on it but there was something about her purposeful stride. For a brief moment, his personal definition of sexy, black woman had appeared in the flesh. Dan had even imagined that he could smell her perfume from the distance. He gathered his wits and continued toward the restaurant doors.

Synz gripped a Raspberry-colored Beret that she wore, and pulled her black wool coat snuggly, as she battled a gust of wind and made her way to the door. Once inside of the building, she went over to a row of elevators. She saw that a car was on the way down. When the doors opened, Synz stepped inside and pushed the button for the floor she wanted. She shoved her hands in pockets and shivered against the cold.

Chapter Eight - The Scale

Dan went into Sara Scales. It was a cozy place that specialized in seafood. The only thing he liked better than to make money was fresh, juicy lobster. The inside of the restaurant had soft gaslights that lined the walls next to each leather covered booth. A waiter greeted him and escorted him to a table by a large bay window. When the server arrived, he was intently looked out of the window.

He had hoped to catch a glimpse of the woman from the cab. The waiter walked over and asked for Daniel's order. Dan ordered a Rock Lobster Platter. The moment the waiter walked away, Dan turned his attention back to the window. Something about the woman from cab had him on edge. Dan idly picked at the linen tablecloth and resumed his watch for another glance of her.

It was nearly thirty minutes later when Dan saw when she came out. She had a bundle wrapped in a receiving blanket. She wasn't alone. A thick, curvy woman gave her a hug and they chatted briefly. Dan reached into his pocket and quickly peeled off three fifties and rushed out of the restaurant. He stood on the sidewalk and looked up and down the street for her. It seemed she had vanished into thin air.

Dan cursed under his breath. He waited and searched for a few more minutes before he'd headed to his room for the night. As soon as he made his way into the room, he took off his jacket and hung it up. He turned on the air-conditioner and flopped down of the bed. Dan closed his eyes and saw her face. His right hand roamed down to his crotch.

He groaned out loud. Dan realized what he'd almost done and stopped. He put his hands behind his heard and turned toward the dresser mirror. The thump in his loins increased. He finally propped up on his elbow and gripped his now fully hard tool through his pants. Dan stared at his reflection in the mirror.

"I wonder what she would think of this."

Dan was in no mood to jack off. He reluctantly slid off the bed and headed for the shower to cool off. When he finished he slipped into a khaki-colored outfit. He glanced in the mirror before he ran his hands over his face. He decided to go to lobby and have a drink.

Dan left the hotel room and paused. His lungs could barely take in oxygen. His hands clenched and his chest heaved as he raised his hand to eyes and rubbed them. He watched her lick her lips for what seemed like an eternity to him. Synz slid an envelope into her purse then went in the room two doors down from his.

He stepped back in his room and closed the door. Dan was surprised that she was in the same building. He sat on the bed and cupped his head in his hands. The opportunity he had hoped for had presented itself. He decided to prop a chair in the door and wait. Dan wanted to ask her out.

Dan was about to doze off when he heard a door slam. He sat upright in the chair and tried regain his poise. He jumped up from the chair; he waltzed out into the hall just in time. She was headed for the elevator. He stepped quickly and stood in front of the doors. He wiped his mouth and tried to speak to her. His clothes were a wrinkled mess from the chair nap.

"Excuse me. How are you doing?" he said.

Synz looked him up and down. Her delicate hand came up and covered her nose. He tilted his head and inhaled. Dan caught a whiff of his breath and held his head down. She realized she had mortified him and smiled to disarm the tension.

When he saw her smile, he shuffled nervously from one foot to the other. His heart melted like warm butter and he felt a tingly sensation in his tummy. She reached into her pocket and pulled out a mint. She opened it and put it up to his mouth. Dan parted his lips and sucked it in. For a brief second she let her finger remain on his lip. Electricity jolted through him.

For the first time, a woman made Dan's insides turn into mush. He reached down to touch her hand and she pulled away. He rubbed his hands together fretfully. Dan swallowed hard before he'd found the courage to open his mouth again.

"Would you like go out to dancing or something?" he blurted out.

"No thank you."

"Can I get your number?"

"I'm flattered, but I can't."

"Can't or won't?"

The elevator door opened. Synz stepped around him and slid into the elevator. He stood there rigid as if frozen in time. His feet wouldn't move. Just as he heard the doors began to close she spoke.

"Have a nice night."

Dan raced to the next elevator bay and pushed the button repeatedly. When the next elevator arrived he slapped the lobby button with force. Dan rubbed the palm of his hand where he had slammed it into the panel of buttons. By the time he was able to walk into the lobby, he saw her get into a small car with another woman. When the car pulled away a few seconds later, Dan huffed with frustration.

He watched as they pulled away from the curb. Dan clasped his hands together and decided to hail a cab. A few moments later a car pulled up into the driveway. The young man had a thick Columbian dialect.

"Where to?" the driver asked.

"Follow that car and please don't lose it."

He turned on the meter and pulled away from the curb. They followed the car through the traffic as it wound its way uptown. He asked the driver to hang back a little. The driver looked at Dan in the rearview mirror suspiciously.

They were a block behind when the car pulled into a driveway in a residential area. He asked the driver to pull over and let him out.

Chapter Nine - Hooked

He paid the fare and began to walk up the street. When he arrived she had already gone into a white wood framed house. Dan was about to knock on her door, when he heard someone cry out. Alarmed she might be in danger he headed for the side of her house to peer into window. Dan gasped at what he saw. She had a light brown skinned female bent over in a blue thong. She was paddling her. He felt a bulge grow in his pants.

He was mesmerized, as he watched her run her hand up the crack of the other woman's back door. He shuddered and vibrated. When he saw Synz's bend down, he unzipped his pants. Dan began touch himself while he peeked through her window, as Synz's kissed the young woman.

Dan didn't blink as she told the woman to get on her knees. When the woman buried her face into Synz twin mounds, he wished it was him. He felt the urge to crawl through the window and kiss her lips for himself. He couldn't stand the pressure and pulled his shaft out.

He heard her scold the woman.

"You still want to be someone's slave? Didn't I tell you no? Now taste what you've been begging for. What's wrong? Don't pull away; lick it."

He began to stroke his shaft while Synz ground her chocolate buns in the women face. She reached behind herself and grabbed the girl' hair. A wig flew through the air. Synz's gripped the short curls on her scalp and continued to discipline her. His focused narrowed to the profile of her lips as he burst a warm load that ran down his leg.

The orgasm was more intensive than usual for him. He leaned on the side of the building to recover. Dan tiptoed back around to the front door. He debated whether he should disturb her. Dan decided to leave instead to go shower.

He tried to memorize the number on the house. 4120 Wabash St. He walked up to Grand River and hailed a cab. When he finally got one to slow down, he asked to go back to the hotel. He hopped in and rode quietly.

"Leaving your woman's house?" The driver asked.

"No, the woman of my dreams and she won't even talk to me."

"She doesn't like you?"

"I don't know yet. I'm hoping she will. "

"Hang in there, she might."

The minute he was back in his room, he wrote down her address in notepad. He wanted to come back to see her. Dan showered, just as the sun had begun to rise over the one of the most beautiful cities in the world. He closed his eyes as the warm water ran over his chiseled frame. He felt that stir in his loins once again that he had at her window.

He immediately made up his mind to go the distance to please her, if he could ever find her again. Dan had to get back home. There was so much work to do. He wanted to be the most successful man he could be. His father's absence in his life had left a deep seated need to prove his worth. For most of Dan's adult life, he had measured his value in dollars. Synz became the first woman that had ever made Dan think of anything other money in a longtime. As soon as his plane landed, at the John Fitzgerald Kennedy Terminal, he bought a postcard.

The first thing Dan did when he made it to his condominium in New York was check his schedule. He wanted to see when he could get back to Detroit. Every weekend that he could find open he penciled in "Detroit". Dan was determined to get back there and find her. It was mid-February the next year, before he returned.

On the second day of February, Synz moved into a three leveled home on Detroit's west side. Synz woke early one morning a week after she moved in. She sat up and clutched her chest. Little

Anthony screamed. She picked the baby from the bassinet beside her bed then headed for the kitchen sink with the fussy baby. Synz rocked him gently until he laid his head on her shoulder and quieted down.

"Just a few more days and we'll get you to where you're supposed to be." Synz said.

Chapter Ten- No Love Lost

Valentines' Day came and went without much fanfare for Synz. She'd attended a Poetry reading at Alvin's near Wayne State University. The club was an avenue for local poets to perform their work in front of an audience. Occasionally, a traveler or two caught wind of the event and came to perform. That night a guest from Rockford, Illinois had moved the crowd with a Dante' styled poem about a girl that he loved.

Just as the last performer for the night took the stage a man walked up to the table and asked Synz if she minded if he sat. Synz looked around and saw that club was crowded. She shrugged her shoulders and turned her attention back to stage. He took a seat quietly.

Synz left shortly before the show was over. She was almost home, when she noticed a dark car tailed her. The vehicle slowed up a bit and then sped up past her down the street. She pulled up into the gateway. The darkness made it difficult to see who was behind the wheel. Except for the outline of a head, it was shadowy inside the car. It stirred her curiosity. The car pulled to the stop sign at the end of her block and tapped the brakes. She rolled up the gate to resident's private back entrance. The complex had two entrances.

Just as she rolled down the window, she noticed the plates were not the standard state colors. She assumed one of her neighbors had out of town guests and went on to her house. She stopped and picked up the mail from the box to sort out later. She threw her keys on the bar. Wise, her little teacup Yorker ran up and practicality jumped into her arms.

He barked emphatically. She rubbed his head and carried him upstairs with her. She saw the cleaning boy had been there. He was a client that came to clean the house at least twice a month. He claimed the guard at the gate flirted with him, he'd thought it was a woman.

She undressed and left a trail of clothes lay strewn about, all the way to the room. Synz slipped into bed and didn't wake until morning. She went to the mailbox to get her mail. There was a car similar to the one from the night before. On the spur-of-the-moment, up she went back into the house to her bedroom.

She dipped her hand inside her Queen Anne nightstand, to bring back the heirloom that she had inherited from her grandmother. The small, pearl-handled, thirty-eight Midnight Special gave her a sense of protection. She reached down into a dark grape Crown Royal satchel that held it away from eyes. Synz waked over to the window and she peeked through the Venetian blinds.

A well-dressed man crossed the lawn to the front door. She checked the chamber and made her way down the stairs. She stood off to the side of the door with the piece pointed towards it when he knocked. Synz peeked and saw the man from the casino lobby.

"Who is it?" She asked.

"I'm looking for the woman from the club last night."

"You have the wrong house."

"No I don't."

"I've told you, you have the wrong house."

"I believe this is the right house."

"I don't know you. I want you off my property. Leave before I call the police."

"Then call the police at least I'll get to see you. It's just a second of your time," he said.

"What do you want? Do have a name?"

"Daniel Davies. I just wanted to ask one question face-to-face without you biting my head off," he said.

She decided to hear him out. The firearm lessons that she had taken to get a weapons permit came in handy. Synz didn't remove the chain, but she cracked the door. She got a good look at his face.

"What?"

"May I come in?"

"No. What do you want?"

Dan looked bewildered and tried to smile.

"Well Ms. Lady, I tried to get to know you last night but you shot me down. I was wondering if maybe we could get together sometimes."

"No"

"Why not?"

"Get the hell off my porch. I don't have to explain myself to you."

He heard the click then turned and walked back to his car. She watched to be sure he pulled off and went to get a cup coffee. That was part of her morning ritual. Synz called the Guard Booth and complained that no one called before a guest had been allowed in. The man that answered said no one had been to the gate and asked for her.

Around lunchtime the guard called to tell her of a delivery. It wasn't uncommon for something to show up that had been ordered as far back as six weeks before. She looked out and saw a white van. There was a young light skinned guy with a huge batch of yellow roses on his way up to the door. She opened the door cautiously.

"Can I help you?" She asked.

"Ms. Synclaire Welch?"

Synz was mystified to who knew her real name except for family. She locked the door and went in and grabbed her Louis Vuitton purse and found a five dollar bill to tip with. Synz went back to take the flowers. She smiled when she opened the card to read it.

"I'm addicted already so how do I get a fix? Let's be friends. Yours Always, Dan".

She started to throw them away. Synz didn't like the thought of a stranger to have sent her gifts. The flowers stunned her and she decided to keep them. Synz had met some unusual characters, but something about him seemed familiar. She went in the dining room and found a vase for the flowers, covered the bottom in water, and put them on the table. She leaned over and smelled them. Synz blushed at the romantic gesture, as she took one sniff of the sweet delicate fragrances.

One of the down sides to be a Mistress for Synz was no companion. There was no one to come home to. She had the submissive will from a partner. The patience and forgiveness of a human heart wasn't there. She'd lined up performances for the night. There was a place she wanted to visit before the performance.

Chapter Eleven - Back Stage Pass

When Synz returned home later that evening, she stayed long enough to pick up a change of clothes. In ten minutes Synz was headed to the Palace out in Southfield. When she pulled up at the house, Synz pulled out her key and took a briefcase from behind her seat. She got out of the car and went in through the side door.

The door eased open and her client was ready in boxer's shorts and tie. He was in the chair and waited as told. Synz closed the door and laid her briefcase on the bed. The client began to wipe the palm of his hands on his boxer shorts as he watched her open the case.

Synz reached inside and produced and ball of tightly wound material. Synz unraveled it and began to tie and bind him with multicolored rainbow silk scarves. After he was secured, she pushed him to his knees with her hand on his shoulder. He whimpered. She stood before him and opened her coat. He swallowed hard at the sight of her in a black skintight latex dress with black open toe spiked heels. Synz wore a black thong underneath it.

The dress was low cut in the front her nipples were almost visible. She went in her briefcase and pulled out white handkerchief, a blindfold, and a leather cat-o-nine whip with small spiked beads. She brought back a ball muzzle for him to bite on and muffle his screams. She gave him the handkerchief to hold on to.

The fabric would hit the floor if the pain became too much. That would stop the session. She blindfolded him and he opened his mouth impatiently for the ball gag. He held his head down, so she could fasten it securely behind his head. Synz walked behind him, she poked him through the open slat in the chair.

"Get up," she said.

He scrambled to his feet reluctantly. The fabric lay ever so delicately in his tied hands.

"Have you been a bad boy? Are you sorry for what you have done?"

He hesitantly shook his head yes. She walked behind him and yanked his head back to bring her lips close to his ear.

"I don't think you are. You wanted to defile me didn't you and rub your hands all over my skin? Maybe even put your tongue off into my precious box and taste me? You think you can buy whatever you want don't you? You couldn't come wouldn't buy schoolbooks for these kids but you got money for this? They're going to need computers and spaceships for this. You deserve to get your ass beat and you know it don't you? "

She shook his head violently up and down for him and he whined in dizzy delight.

She stood behind his sightless, gagged slab of flesh, a frosty wave of coldness flowed through her when she flexed her wrist. The whip came twirled through the air from her actions. The first blow landed across his bareback. With firm elegant swings, she lashed out over and again.

(Synz delusion was that of a small eight years old female. The girl held a whip while music played inside her head with beats from drums made long ago. She felt an encouraged sense of justice for the bodies that lay on the ground. A screaming mother wailed at the shore for the return of her children in the distance. The echoing sound of heavy footsteps from men approaching to protect their home from further invasion swelled closer in the girl's ears. All far as she could see, there was a gruesome scene of hurt and destruction at the village shore. An ancestral chant voices filled her from within. She reared her hand back again, firmly clutching the handle of the whip.)

Silently, so she didn't miss a whimper, mutter, or slap Synz whipped him. She tried to calculate every swing to heighten the damage. She rolled him over and straddled him to remove the blindfold. There was shame in his eyes and a tiny spark. The sight of her face changed his mood. She smelled fear seep from his pores.

"Bad woof woof." Synz mumbled.

The something from the light called her and she began to twist the ends his tie. For a brief while she sat there and ground her warm body box on his pole through material of his shorts. She felt wetness between them and jumped up to shower. She left him lain out on the floor, when she returned twenty minutes later, he was asleep. Synz rolled him on his side into a fetal position.

She gently untied his wrists and pried the material from his hands. Quietly, she packed her case she left. Synz opened the door and walked back to the side door. After a quick search both ways down the driveway she slipped out into the night and returned to her car.

Synz strapped her in and adjusted her rear-view mirror. She pulled into the Southfield traffic. She drove until she saw the I-696 entrance. Synz had one more stop before she went home.

"Synclaire."

When she turned to look around the car, no one was there. Synz reasoned it was her imagination. Synz couldn't shake the sense that someone did call her name. Something had made her uneasy. Synz pulled out into traffic on Thirteen Mile up to the first red light to hop onto the freeway to go home. It was time to plan her well-deserved voyage somewhere. She didn't like to feel the need to peek around corners and through blinds and it wasn't her style. Great paranoia surrounded her, unlike anything she had known before. More importantly Synz rarely gave in to fear.

She arrived home twenty minutes later and keyed in the code for the gate to open. After she'd headed down the main driveway to her door, she checked the mirror and once again saw a dark car. Annoyed, she rolled back to confront the driver. The car sped into reverse and disappeared into the night. The tension had built up within her. The pit of her stomach growled.

Chapter Twelve- The price

Synz was twenty-two, lived on her own, and had long tired of her own meager attempts to cook. She woke up hungry from her nap and decided to go out in search of food. Synz slipped on her shoes, grabbed her keys and went out of the car. Once inside the vehicle she turned on the ignition and headed out to Ye Old Subshoppe.

She pulled up into the parking lot and sat for a moment. Through the restaurant glass she could see that it was empty with the exception of one employee behind the counter. He appeared to be quite attractive. Synz cut the car off and went in.

She walked up to the counter and placed her order. She folded her arms and paced while the employee made her sandwich. The person behind the counter stopped and stretched. Synz saw the outline of a defined body and muscles.

When her order was up, Synz watched as her food was shoved into a bag and the employee rung up the total. Synz moved over to the register and dug through her purse. She found a piece of twenty dollar bill and pen. She passed the currency through the open slot. The cashier took the money and gave her the balance and a receipt. Synz took the money and slip of paper and then scribbled her number on the back of the receipt. Afterwards, Synz reached into the carousel window for her food and put her number in its place. She glanced over at the name tag on the shirt of the person behind the window.

"If you're not otherwise committed Alex, then call me sometimes. My name is Synz." Synz said.

Synz left the restaurant and made her way back to her house. She hadn't given more thought to Alex. Her cell phone rang while she ate. Synz let it go to voicemail. After she was done, she'd thought to return the call. She called the number on her screen and waited.

"Ye Old Subshoppe," Alex said.

"Did someone call Synz?"

"Yeah, this is Alex. What you doing tomorrow night?"

"Spending it with you I hope."

"That's what's up. Can you meet at me about five thirty? I can fix you something to eat and maybe watch a movie or something?"

"Word up, sexy."

They agreed and just that easy the plan was on. She felt like it could be an adventure. Alex wanted to pass as a male to the world and Synz's didn't mind. The more Synz thought about it the more she wanted to have her. She could barely rest, as she thought about then dreamed about her and Alex that night.

In Synz's' dream, her and Alex kissed, giggled, held hands, and strolled along the Detroit River Walk and chatted about what might be on the other side of the moon; they both fell deeply in love, while they stared across the water and the Canadian skyline. Synz had a romantic notion of what they could've been, before it ever started.

Right in the middle of a long soulful kiss the alarm on her nightstand went off. Synz's wanted plenty of time to get her gear on and look good. She set her alarm to go off an hour before she needed to be up. It was important to her to be at her best. The bed was so warm and cozy, she found it hard to let go of the mattress.

She'd made her way to bathroom to get ready for the day. After she had bathed, Synz slathered her body with a Peach Bloom bath set and baby oil and got dressed. It took some time get it altogether. She found a bottle of perfume that one of her sister had left behind. She called and asked Lily for something a little fancier than cotton panties to put on. Lily had doted on Synz's from the first day she came home from the hospital.

Synz's arrived at Lilly's house a little while later. They settled on a black Teddy with a royal purple panel in the front that closed like a corset with a set of black thigh hi's. Synz tried it on in the bathroom so she could see in the big mirror behind the door. Synz was pleased that her body looked delicious from head to toe. She came out to see Lily stand in the hall.

"Damnnn that's hot. You better take your fast behind to college or something. You'd best grow up to be something to go with all that sexy. I don't want you to mess that up. Maybe one day you'll teach me some of that old fancy stuff you be dreaming up. You have quite the imagination. I still remember when you dressed up in my clothes and pretended to be She-Ra, queen of the universe. You insisted that everyone call you by your "super-hero" name. You're getting too big for that now, if you're going to move into the sex game that is." Lily said.

"I'm going. I remember when a counselor came to school and told us that there was a big difference in the way our lives could turn out with a degree. I want to go college. I'm not sure what I want to be but I'm going," Synz replied.

"The best you can do for all of us, is taking that attitude somewhere it's useful. I'm serious and I'm telling you straight up, you don't want to follow in my steps. I cared more about what a man thought about me, than I did worrying about my future. You don't have any idea what I've been through having a baby this young. My daughters' father was gone off to the next chick before I even gave birth to her. I'm left to be both mother and father. It ain't easy. "

Chapter Thirteen - Two of Hearts

Synz's didn't respond, instead she kissed her sister, before she changed clothes and stuck the outfit in her book bag then left. Synz's wondered if anyone else noticed, her once vibrant sister had become a thin pale version of herself. She was fidgety and most of the time barely slept or ate. Her gorgeous face had started to sink in and her eyes had deep dark circles around them. She used to shop nonstop, but lately she didn't have any extra money.

The next day, Synz went about her business as usual. She'd wanted to ask her sister was she okay, but thought better of it. Synz didn't want her to feel as if she was only there to pry. Besides, in her mind her sister might be embarrassed by her questions. It was four in the afternoon when she'd remembered her date with Alex. She rushed home, packed her bag and went out and put it in the back seat of the car. Synz went back inside and called Alex. Alex gave her the address and Synz told her she'd be there in half an hour.

When Synz arrived at Alex's house, Alex had come outside to the driveway to meet her. Inside the foyer and everywhere else she looked was beautiful hardwood and marble trim. It had been decorated straight from a page of the Good Homes and Gardens magazine. The entire interior had been decorated with style and elegance. The dining room table was set with fine China. A vase full of fresh lilacs and baby breaths decorated the table.

Alex led Synz upstairs to the bedroom and gave her a quick tour of the house. She told her that her great-grandparents had bought the property more than fifty years ago. It currently belonged to her mother. Her Mom had left to train in preparation for the Gulf War. She talked about how proud she was of her mother's readiness to fight for her country.

When they finally made it to her room, Alex went over to a stack of tapes on her dresser to pick out a movie.

"Hey, I got this movie from the Flea Market the other day but I haven't watched it," Alex said.

"What it is?" Synz asked.

"Our Art, I'm not sure what it's about, but the guy said he could barely keep a copy, so it must be good. Here check it out."

Synz read the back cover with curiosity. She sat at the foot of the bed while

Alex put the movie on. After the movie came on, Synz watched Alex out of her side view more than the movie. Night had come and Synz's decided to make a play for her. As she lay back across the bed on propped arms, she'd waited. Alex seemed preoccupied. When Synz's excused herself to the bathroom for a shower, she grabbed her back pack. In the privacy of the bathroom she showered then slipped back into the Teddy. She came out and saw a rainbow striped boxer shorts and a white top lay out on the bed. Alex held out a sparkly gold gift bag towards her.

"Look baby I got something for you," she said.

She opened it to find a genuine Chinese robe from Macy's.

"Thank you, it's beautiful. I wasn't expecting anything so I didn't bring you anything."

"You don't have to give me anything or do anything. I saw it and decided it would look good on you. So I got it."

She stepped up and kissed Alex on the cheek. Alex smiled shyly and grabbed her clothes from the bed and quickly went in the bathroom. Synz's waited until the bathroom door closed. She took off the tee shirt and put it on the robe. The fabric felt sexy to her against her chocolate skin. She crawled in the bed and lay down on cool satin sheets. When the door opened Alex stood there in a matched housecoat. She jumped on the bed and started a pillow fight.

"Hold on now babe, I don't play fight," Synz's said.

She rarely played games and didn't see the pillow as it headed towards her, but before Synz's could protest more, Alex had done it again. She caught it and snickered while she tried to wrestle the pillow away. Somehow she managed to pin her down and straddle her. They both laughed.

"Stop it," she said.

Alex ignored her and quickly reversed it so she was now on top of her. She reached up and grabbed the back of her almost bald head and pulled her face down. A current pulsed through them when their lips touched. Synz's slowly slid her legs apart and started to grind her hips. Synz had never been with a girl; however the desire to respond to Alex as if she were a boy somehow came naturally to her.

She found herself aroused. Alex breathed in her ear like a bull in a rage. Whatever the game was it went straight out the window. Synz's slid her hand down towards Alex's crotch. She was curious to know what Alex felt like. When Alex realized what she was up to she stopped her and rolled off the bed.

"I don't know who you've been with Synz but I don't want or need that. Lay back and let me do what I do."

Alex reached across Synz and turned off the light. Except for the soft bluish glow of the TV it was dark in the room. Synz's asked for some music and Alex turned the radio to one hundred and seven and a half.

"Thanks for tuning in," a soulful voice said.

Chapter Fourteen- Who is that

A song called "When Doves Cry" started to play and romanced filled the air as Alex placed her arm on the pillow besides Synz's head, then rose up to rest lightly on top of Synz. Alex let her free-hand travel along Synz's side and rest on her ample hip. Synz parted her lips slightly to protest but immediately felt Alex's tongue probe them, before she could get a word out. She tensed up when Alex's fingers began to roam her body and she felt her fingers touched the middle of her Teddy. She rose slightly and slipped her way down to Synz's crotch. The heat from her breath left a warm sensual trail across her thigh.

Alex started kiss her skin and made her way slowly over the fabric down to her hottest spot. Synz mind raced but she was curious about what Alex was about to do. Alex finally opened the snaps and exposed Synz's' delicate treasures. Her tongue licked at Synz's moist lips before she'd parted them with her gently with her fingers. Synz gasped a little when Alex's soft wet tongue dipped down and glided a trail along the inside fold.

Her warm, easy tongue brushed a slow and lazy wet path around the rim of her labia before Alex sucked her button into her mouth. Alex licked upward just enough to pin down Synz clitoris with her tongue and then teased it into complete stiffness. She licked lovingly all around the button until it throbbed like it had a heartbeat. Synz gasped softly, as she wondered if Alex had done this before. At that moment, it didn't matter, what Alex had done with her body, it was something Synz knew she definitely liked.

While she groaned from a special place deep inside, Synz legs stiffened up. Repeatedly, she felt her body tense up to the point of near-spasms. Alex waited until she felt Synz shiver and then change the pace or pressure of her tongue strokes. Whenever Alex did, Synz resisted the urge to cry out in frustration. Alex rocked her hips as she abandoned her resolve to go slowly. Alex had resisted the fall into the flow as long as she could. Alex grabbed Synz's thighs and firmly held her in place and gently sucked on her love button firmly. Synz reached down and instinctively ground her box into Alex's face. A few minutes' later waves of pleasure to finish with a final tide that seemed as if it washed over Synz's entire body. Alex lapped from her until she was nearly delirious. The room had started to spin and Synz lungs felt like she was trapped in a void as the final ripple passed through her.

She wrapped her thighs around Alex's back and let it go until her body relaxed in exhaustion. She had set off a reaction and Alex came too. Synz laid-back and tried to catch her breath as Alex pulled up onto her. Alex fumbled around near her own waist for a moment in the dark, while Synz rested.

"If you take that kind of loving from me, I might go crazy. Am I supposed to do something for you? I mean I don't know how to ummm… this is my first time." Synz said.

"You're first time ever or getting ate out?" Alex asked.

"That too."

"Oh, you mean the first time ever?"

"Yes. I'm glad it happened this way."

"I didn't know. I guess we should've talked first huh?"

"No. its fine, it's just that I didn't know what to expect."

"I'm a giver."

"What does that mean?"

"I'm the one that likes to do the pleasing. I don't care for anyone touching all on me in a girly-ass way. I like girls like you that just receive pleasure. I don't date aggressive women."

"So, I'm the receiver?"

"Yeah or femme, meaning girl lesbian, whatever you decide you're comfortable with as your role."

"I don't have a role. I just know I like this the way you're doing it. If I'm the receiver though how do you…umm you know. How do I make you feel like as good as I do?"

"By letting me. I get off from getting you off. I love the way you scratch and claw at me when I'm in you. That shit turns me on. I feel like at that moment, you complete me for a while and let me feel like I'm your man. It's everything from the sounds you make to the way your body reacts to my touch."

"Okay, so I want if I wanted to try and ummm taste you?"

"Well, I don't really care to be the one on the pillow. There is something you can do for me though."

"What's that?"

"Lie back and let me finish."

Synz opened her arms. Alex crawled back on top of Synz's and handled her tight slot. A moment later, Alex pushed into her soaked box with a strap-on dildo. Synz's' body shuddered and vibrated before she loosened the grip on her thighs. Alex hands grabbed her cheeks on both sides. Alex dug under her, while Synz rose just enough for her to grip her firmly. When Synz felt the pressure against her lips, she stiffened up. Slowly Alex slid into her. Synz winced as she felt a dull pain. Synz bit down on Alex's shoulder as continues to break through inside of her.

At first Alex went at a delicate pace. The friction of the dildo inside her tight walls was a curious sensation to Synz. She closed her eyes tightly until the pressure began to subside. Suddenly, Alex began to increase the pace of her strokes. When Alex pulled Synz leg up, she felt her body loosened and Alex slid even deeper inside her.

Synz groaned as she her body began to nurse of the firm tool lodged in her. The erotic moan from Synz's lips while so close to Alex's ear seemed to excite Alex.

With an increased fervor, Alex exploded so long and hard her eyes saw a colorful streak from the light through tears streamed down her face. Alex had fantasized many nights, to take a woman with as if she were a man. The mere thought that Alex was the first to touch Synz's womb, had sent her into a realm of sexual thoughts that Alex had never dared to think before. Synz sweet kisses and tender touch brought Alex back to the reality, as she tried to hide her tears.

Chapter Fifteen - Payless

Alex leaned forward and sighed into the soft crease of her neck. Synz wiggled her hips. Alex took a deep breath and slid back out of Synz half-way. While released the air Alex plunged back into Synz's warm body. Synz reared her hips towards Alex. When Synz threw her leg up, Alex doubled the pace of her short strokes. Alex pushed up on her arms when Synz legs began to tremble. Synz bit hard down on her bottom lip and whimpered while she felt an intense urgency filled her loins. Synz began to claw at Alex's back as she experienced her first dick-induced orgasm. The tiny chocolate woman that squirmed under her was yet another portion of her fantasies come true and she burst again.

Alex brushed her lips across Synz's juicy thick bottom lip. She nibbled her way back down Synz's body to her triangle center. She experienced a second tremor when Alex abruptly pulled out, slid down and started to gently taste Synz again. Whatever man Alex had looked up would have been proud of her skills. Synz was exhausted.

They dozed off and cuddled in each other's arms. Synz's awoke first and moved to sit up but couldn't. Alex was asleep but Synz felt something pressure against her thigh. Aroused, she manipulated her body to try to reach out and touch it. She had never seen a dildo before and she was curious enough to peek.

Alex awoke and began to nibble on her neck. She ran her fingers over Synz's fat mound and began to tease her. Alex crawled on top of her. It was almost inside when Synz's began wiggle her hips. She threw her leg and draped her foot across one of Alex's shoulders again. Alex smiled, when she realized that because she'd been the first to pleasure Synz with her tongue, that Synz wasn't familiar with many positions. Alex braced her arms on both sides of the pillow before she thrust her hips and slid into Synz again.

Alex's arms stiffened while she struggled to keep some sense of control over her weight and motions. Synz saw quickly that Alex could be delicate or rough with each stroke. Synz had begun to try to concentrate and countered every move that Alex made. Alex stared straight at the headboard. She had hoped that if she stared ahead, instead of at Synz, then she could control the passion that grew in her.

When at last Alex looked down at Synz's face and made eye contact, with flared nostrils, she drove into her. Alex's eyes turned hazel and for the first time Synz's noticed the sparks in them. She sucked in a deep breath and tried to relax.

"I want you. I love being deep in you." Alex said.

Her eyes glazed over a bit and she let out a moan that sounded like a hungry wolf's growl. Synz's felt juices roll down her thigh. They were gone in a flash and the flow with release. Alex buried her face inside Synz's box.

They exchanged a few short kisses before she made her way to the bathroom to shower. Synz's decided to have a bath over a shower and ran warm water in the bath tub to ease into. She let a sigh of relief out as she lowered herself down into the water for a few minutes. Her mind wandered over the way Alex had made love to her. The water had begun to cool as she washed herself. It was nearly six thirty am, when she finished. Synz took a towel and came out. Alex was stretched out across the bed and watched Scooby-Doo. Synz kissed Alex before she got dressed. Alex rolled off the bed and headed to shower as well. By a quarter after seven they were dressed and headed in different directions to school.

Synz's looked for pictures of her younger years on the way out. Awards and trophies decorated the room but few pictures. She decided it was odd but let it go. Alex hadn't talked much about her youth and Synz never asked.

For the next few years they were lovers. They had made plans to spend the evening together the next day when Alex got off work. Synz's took a cab to her job to meet her. She got out of the cab and went in to get Alex. When she walked through the door a female named Fabian from around the way got in her face. The broad had a reputation that preceded her.

The store was empty and she noticed the woman didn't have any food in her hands as she walked toward the door. Alex smiled until she'd noticed that Synz stood there. Her eyes narrowed as she approached her.

She wasn't in a position to curse Alex out. Their trysts were something they had kept mostly private. She cocked her head to the side when she'd heard Fabian flirt. There was a snide undertone in her words.

"I just love the way you say that." Fabian said as she walked out of the door.

"What was that about?" Synz asked.

"Nothing, so don't trip."

"Yeah, okay well guys hit on me all the time. Maybe I should enjoy the company of a man for a little while, see how you feel."

"That's what you want? Is that what you see in Leanne, is she manlier?"

"Who is Leanne?"

"You tell me? I was at Splash's for karaoke when someone mentioned they saw you coming out of the Alpine Hotel with Leanne."

"Is that so? Why didn't you ask me? So anyone can just walk up to you and say I did something? I guess your friends run our relationship. You're too old to be that damn silly."

"That's how you're going to act Synz's? I'm starting to fall in love with you."

"What? I'm not trying to fall in love. I don't want to share you but we have a lot of bridges to cross before we start talking about forever. I'm not really ready for a commitment other than what we're doing right now."

"Oh so you want to play the field first?"

"I'm trying to find where I want to be first, no offense but I'd appreciate it if we could slow down. "

"Yeah whatever Synz, I've seen you put a little twist in your walk because them men was watching before now."

"I've tried to give you everything you wanted, so far it feels like it hasn't been enough."

"Everything I wanted?

"Almost."

"Okay, then how about that juicy behind? You can lie on your side and it won't hurt."

"Hell no."

Chapter Sixteen -Unhinged

Synz's and Alex began to argue in the store. Synz walked out into the parking lot towards the cab and Alex trailed behind her. Alex was incensed that Synz wouldn't give in. They bickered all the way back to Alex's house. Once inside Synz's crawled into the bed and let her have her say. She talked so long that Synz's dozed off.

She woke up to the familiar chirp of a cell phone. She reached out in the dark of a hot and humid Detroit night across her lover's body. The one that just a month prior developed the ability to wake up and check a phone call at 12:18 in the morning.

Their hands landed on the phone at nearly the same time. Synz's touched it first and felt the rough calloused skin of her mate wrap warmly over hers. She heard the gasp as it left her lips. There was tenseness as Alex's strong muscular legs prepared to jump out of bed. Synz's smelled the deliberate release of a mouthful of hot defeated air. It was her first encounter with women's intuition. Something in her gut had set her off.

Her heart pounded, as vivid images of little things that bothered her invaded her thoughts at once. Suspected stories that never quite rang true, that had come from Alex's lips started to click in her head. She flipped back to the third grade all over again as it all played through her mind. The scenes blurred and flew through her head all in a flash. Her earth shook with no more than a ringing sound to warn her.

She rushed her hand away with the phone still in it and ran to the bathroom then locked the door behind her. Her hands trembled. She pulled up the screen and went to the call list and before she could get the list up. The phone rang in her hands.

"Hello" she said.

"Hey baby, I'm just getting off work and my body is hungry for some time with you," a female said.

Synz's hung up. She wanted to know but she didn't feel her heart could handle it since she loved Alex. She didn't want to hear it because it would mean she had been blind. It overwhelmed her to sit there and accept it. The slap of betrayal caused the tears to pour.

Synz's began to quake from head to toe from within so hard her bones rattled. Anger flushed through her and warmth rushed to her cheeks. She snapped. A sense of eerie calm washed over her and something in her oozed out through the giant split in her soul.

"Why does this hurt so much?" She wondered.

The phone lit up again in her palm as it trembled. Her heart thumped wildly inside of her. She stripped and stepped in the shower. Afterwards, she turned on the hot water to subdue the coldness that crept into her. Alex knocked on the bathroom door and called her name to no avail for nearly fifteen minutes. When Synz was finished with her shower she opened the door wrapped in a towel with the phone in her hand. Alex was there and searched Synz's face for a reaction.

Tears streamed down Synz's face as she exited the bathroom. Alex didn't notice the twisted look that was on her face underneath those tears. Synz clicked on a lamp to see her way around the bedroom, before she snatched up her bag and began to grab lingerie and personal items. Synz packed her things quickly.

"Baby wait, please let me explain," Alex said.

"Tell me why?"

"Revenge at first, I was sure that you had screwed Leanne when I slept with Fabian. Then I saw the girl that my friend had pointed the week before when I at the pool hall. I asked the woman and then she said her name wasn't even Leanne. Fabian was paid me and you got most of the money. She even tried to propose to me with a cheap ass mood ring."

"So you're a gigolo?"

"No Synz it wasn't like that."

"I'm not going to be faithful to someone who cheats on me. It's not like this is the only lie anyway."

Her mouth fell open and Synz watched her brain absorb the shock and try to form words at the same time. Synz's up her hand up in a manner that could only mean silence and hurled theirs pictures, cards, and her magic egg vibrator into the bag and zipped it. She threw her pride in the bag and took that too. The bag was slung across her shoulder like a robber with a pocketful of money.

Alex trailed behind Synz and tried to find the words to get her to talk.

"So you're just going to leave me huh? After all this time Synz, come on now girl. She means nothing to me and you are the only woman I have ever loved. I made a mistake. I do love you, so don't do this. Talk to me baby. No one will ever love you like I do. Ok, that's not the best choice of words. Please don't do this to us. Are you coming back or is this goodbye? Please honey, say something. "

"Why? What do you mean do this to us? Was she nothing when you fucked her or did you call her baby too?"

Synz walked down the stairs and out of the house without another word. It was almost four o'clock in the morning. She desperately wanted to call her sisters but didn't want to explain why she was at Alex's house in the first place. Her mind was blown from the shock to have caught Alex. Synz put her hand over her mouth to keep in her desire to scream out into the dark.

She got in her car and drove down to the Twenty Grand in the dark to wait until she could get it together. The place was a source of comfort when she was younger. She remembered her trips there on her lunch time with her girlfriends from school several years prior. The restaurant was opened twenty four hours. Synz went in to the counter and asked for a hot chocolate. Synz paid for the beverage and waited on her change. After she got her drink, she walked over to the jukebox in the back corner of the restaurant.

Synz dropped two case quarters into the machine and poked in her selections. As she passed the empty tables in search of the most remote one, Synz reached out and grasped a handful of napkins. She had barely sat down when Jerry Butler's "Lies" began to play. Synz put her head down on the table to hide the free flow of her tears.

Chapter Seventeen - 20 Thousand

She yearned to talk to her mother but Synz' was too ashamed. Synz had lied to her mother and hid the nature of her relationship with Alex, for nearly two years. Her mother was the one person that she knew that wanted nothing but the best for her. January would have been upset that Synz had kept this from her, yet she still would have given her whatever support she needed.

Synz wrestled with the urge to call Lily anyway; on the other hand it presented her with the same problem. Both of her sisters had hinted that Synz spent a lot of time and hung out with Alex or talked about her. When the chance came to let them in on her secret love affair, she didn't. She realized they would be pissed with her that she wasn't honest with them either. Then the long-winded lecture would come before either one of them actually worried about how she'd felt.

Synz had trapped herself into an emotional corner, alone with her secret. If Alex didn't know what a diamond was, Synz hoped that Alex would know when she saw her again. She walked around out of her mind for days. She fought with her own inner demons to get past the incident and return to her normal self. Synz hadn't called or seen Alex. She had decided that even with the hurt, the last thing she wanted to do was add insult to injury and try to work anything out with Alex.

A week later her house phone rang, just as she came through the door.

"Hello Welch residence," Synz said.

"Yeah, lick it like that," a female said.

"Damn hold your legs up. You should have shaved first and where is it? You call that a pacifier?" Alex said.

Synz hung up the phone and stood there. The water swelled up in her eyes. She heard something rip into shreds right inside her ears.

Those first few nights without her had been rougher than she'd expected. The missed phone call to simply say goodnight was the worst. The woman in her wanted desperately to at least hear Alex's voice. Regardless of what Alex had done the bond as they explored and grew as a couple didn't break because of another woman. Every woman wants to feel as if they are special when it comes to a lover.

The reality that someone might decide that said woman is not enough can be a bitter pill to swallow. Synz learned that what she'd felt for Alex didn't simply turn off like a water tap. It felt more like the sounds that a faucet would make with air in the pipes. Whenever Synz tried to turn her love on for Alex, it rattled and banged. It had been a difficult choice to avoid her strong desire to fix it. Synz's had resolved to take care of her own heart first.

One morning after the break-up with Alex, she went outside and found that someone had stabbed the back tire. She went to Chuck's tire shop to get it fixed. Two days later, she came out for school and found eggs thrown all over the car. She drove over to Bill's Carwash and had it cleaned. Finally three days after the egg fiasco, her car motor seized up while she drove down Michigan Avenue. She called a tow truck and when it arrived the driver jumped out and he went over to look at it the car.

"Hi, I'm Frank. What's the problem?" the driver said.

"I don't know. I was hoping you could tell me?"

"Try to start it up and let me see what it does."

"Okay"

She tried it again and it got the same results. He raised the hood and tinkered around with it for a while. She sat in the car frustrated. Synz's reached inside the glove compartment and pulled out a book. He walked around the car and opened the gas cap door. She could see him in her side view mirror; he shook his head like something was amiss. At last he walked up to the driver's side door.

"Well?" she said.

"Come here, I want to show you something."

"See that yellow sludge right there?" He said.

"Yeah"

"That's sugar. Your motor froze up because somebody put sugar in your gas tank. This car has a body but you need a different motor. Are you beefing with somebody because that is some hateful shit right here?"

"I've been having some strange stuff happening lately after a break up. I guess her other woman wants to make it personal."

"Did you say her?"

"Yeah, what does that have to do with my car?"

"Nothing I don't have a problem with that. I can tow this back to your house. You can either find another motor for it or sell the body."

"Just take it to my house please."

"Alright you can go ahead and get in the truck, so I can get it loaded. Put the key in the ignition for me okay."

She did as he asked and waited while he hooked the car up. He got in and she gave him the address to her house. She was quiet as she stared out the window tried not to scream out in frustration. They rode in silence.

"How much do I owe you?"

"Nothing"

"Thank you, are you sure we're good on this?"

"Would you go out to dinner with me?"

"What?"

"Keep your money. What do you say? Will you have dinner with me please?"

"Are you single or are you asking me because I mentioned that I'd had a girlfriend?"

"I'm asking because I want to. Can I get your number and call you later then at least?"

"You didn't even ask me if I had a man already."

"Do you?"

"No"

"You're probably going to be my wife and the mother of my kids one day, let's start this off with a little romance."

"I don't know."

"So you're going to make me go find someone else even though I want you? You're bold baby cakes. That's okay. You think I'm playing and I'm serious. Give me a chance."

"You can call me sometimes but I've already told you what I'm on. Don't think this means anything okay?"

"Of course not, I just want to get to know you better."

"You're probably just trying to scheme up on a threesome or something."

"It is about to be my birthday."

"You're a straight up flirt. Call me tomorrow, I need to get in and figure out what I'm going to do."

Chapter Eighteen -Hateful

Synz could feel his eyes on her as she stepped out of the truck. She walked away real slow and went up to the door of the house. When she looked back over her shoulders at him, he licked his soft pink lips. Synz's briefly wondered about the way he'd licked his lips, as she opened the screen door.

She hadn't planned to sleep with him, still her limited sexual experience with men made her curious. Synz didn't know if someone could satisfy her same way Alex had. It had been more a week since Alex had pleasured Synz last. Hormones had started to explore the possibilities, in the depths of Synz's mind.

Synz was sure that Alex hadn't missed any pleasure. The knowledge that there was someone else in Alex's arms was the main thing Synz wanted to hold on to and ignore at the same time. Acknowledgement had kept her from the idea of them as a couple again. Synz thought that if she ignored what had gone on it could mean more heartache. The logic that Alex could have shared her love with another woman at that very moment, allowed her to move on with her own life, as it were. Every ounce of her wanted Alex to take it all back. When Synz woke up in the morning, the place that she preferred to be was nestled in Alex's arms. She missed the way Alex held her from behind and spooned her every night.

Once Synz was inside the house, the suppressed resentment and upset had returned with a fury. Synz felt her rage worsened as she went over the situation mentally. Something inside her heart kept her from out of the fire of pain. Nasty emotions simmered like soup, until she finally let go of her tears and cried. She paced the floor and tried to calm down. She couldn't think of anyone who had a reason go out of their way to damage her car, except Alex. Synz realized that if she called her and asked that Alex might believe she wanted something other than whatever she said. Synz went to bed that night once again with Alex in her thoughts, as she drifted to sleep fitfully.

Early the next day, Synz called Alex to ask how she and her grandmother were anyway. She felt the need to make peace with the issues at hand and bring things to a point of closure. Synz had come to the realization that the next chapter couldn't be written in her life, until she had ended the one with Alex. As she dialed the numbers, she held her breath. When Alex answered, she immediately went into a long tirade about how lonely and unsatisfied she was. Alex launched into an outburst about how she and Synz had shared too much to just walk away. Synz hadn't got a chance to get to the point of her call.

"Just like that huh? I'm supposed to take you back just like that. I saw you wearing that cheap ass ring. You led her on to think it was going to be something between you two. You know you're wrong. As far as my feelings, let me worry about that okay," Synz said.

"I don't want to lose you."

"I don't know what I'm feeling and I don't want to decide right now."

"I've told you for the last time, she was threw money at me baby. I would've been a fool not to drain her for every penny I could get. You demanded so much, I saw her as a meal ticket. I hooked my boys up with her and they hit those pockets too. She only busted that tire when she found out I was still seeing you."

"I never told you anything happened to my car."

"You didn't?"

"It sounds like you were looking for somebody to pay you for your love. You're asking me to be her. No thank you. Money can't buy you love, especially the kind I have for you. How could you do this to us? How do I get back to the point of loving you that way? "

Synz hung up on her. Her conceit wouldn't let her go back to Alex. The pain was still fresh but the trust was broken. On top of wounded pride it now felt as if Alex wanted Synz to somehow fix the mess that had been made of what used to be them.

Synz's had wanted to love Alex. The belief that love could conquer anything that had been Synz's position had wavered. The need to hurt Alex was the furthest thing from Synz mind, but she was mindful that Alex had hurt her. There wasn't a guarantee that given a chance that Alex wouldn't do the same again. Synz had become afraid of Alex's love. Alex confirmed Synz's fear when she turned bitter over the phone a few days later.

"Really Synz, so I hear that you screwed Fable's ex-woman. You were all out in public with her and giggled for her like you did with me. Do you think that your new woman can love you more than I do? Fabian already told me what a loser that girl is. This is some bullshit just to keep up drama between me and Fabian." she asked.

"You know what? You're a trip for real. Why would I care about what you or your girl said? I'll get another car, but you will never get another me. Now, how I get what I used to get from you shouldn't concern either of you. Fabian wanted what I had so badly, now she has it, drama and all. Shouldn't the two of you love up each other, instead of all of this concern about me?"

"If I were ever going to spend my life with a woman it's you. I've never been in a serious relationship and I messed up. I'm sorry."

"I accept your apology. I'm not perfect either, but it hurts too much. If you believe that I'm worth it then do your best."

One week later she got a call from Alex.

"Tell your friends to leave me and Fabian alone. It's clear to me that you're jealous of her. " Alex said.

"I don't know what you are talking about. You and Fable deserve one another. I haven't seen my friends or anyone else for that matter for at least a few months. You better take another look at your new sweetie and question her. Maybe another female you've been with is mad at you, go run to her. I've never noticed how you were always tried to insult and belittle me on the low too. She has a cheater that still wants to get with me, what in the hell do I have to be jealous of? You're supposed to be her man now yet you use any excuse you can to call me. You need someone to talk to about your troubles then call her phone. People piss me off with this dumb shit. It seems I went from the butt of the joke to a solution awfully fast. I thought she had a better idea. I don't think you all have spent enough time on the relationship. Until the two of you are on more solid ground, don't call me. I'm not cut like that. It's been hard to enough to accept it, but I refuse to wallow in it with you or her. " Synz replied.

Chapter Nineteen - Fable

"You're mad that I hurt you. Then on top of everything else, you have the nerve enough to let Fabian's ex get between your thighs."

"No, no, no, this doesn't work like that. I'm free to see other people. You've been exploring, I'm trying to do the same and find what works for me. If for some reason I've spoken to someone that she used to be with, it hasn't been brought to my attention."

"You're not mad at me?"

"Why do you care? It seems as though you're scared that I'm going to find someone that will treat better than you did. Our whole life was based on sex, lies, and betrayal. That's not enough for me, it's not love. I just hate that I loved you."

"So you're saying you don't want me, huh?"

"I love you. A part of me will never forget you."

"I want you in my life, in my bed. Let me love you. I won't ever give this up again. Given a chance I would gladly make this up to you every waking moment of my life. I can't stand the thought you hating me because of Fabian."

"This ain't about Fabian. If she didn't look wore out, like she ain't slept in months, I might have understood. I'd hoped to spend forever with you. I'm not really sure why you keep bringing her name up. This is only about what you and I were supposed to mean to each other. It didn't work out. Still, I won't become a bitter female over you or this. I've lied to everyone including myself, for this thing I thought was love. Now, I see the person I needed to give my love to first is me. Maybe this is the consequences for the wrong I've done. Either way the price is pain and hurt, or suck up the thought that I might need help to love what's supposed to be mine. I'm unwilling to do either. When it is meant to be for me, it won't require for me to lie about or hide it. You want me to fall apart, even though I really don't see exactly what I'd be falling to pieces over. I can't help you feel better about this. I just can't."

Synz pushed the end button on the phone; Synz had to admit that she was still hurt. She assumed that Alex would eventually cheat on Ms. New-booty too. Even though her body was on fire with lust for Alex's touch, Synz only wanted that touch if it was reserved for her alone. She was confident that Alex's mistress would have a turn to drink from the bitter cup of betrayal.

At bare minimum, Alex had already admitted that she still wanted Synz. The statement alone had given Synz a measure of comfort. Synz had decided to take a page from the women in her family. She might even give Fabian a bright smile when she saw her again. After all, Alex's attempt to repair things with her told Synz that, Alex was prepared to hurt Fabian as well.

Synz went into the bathroom and undressed and started her bath water. She'd taken off her jewelry off then placed it in a bowl on the counter. Synz pinned her hair up, before she eased her foot into a warm bubble bath. She bathed and slipped into a soft green Terry cloth robe in the dark. She took one more look through the blinds before she lay down. Two hours later, a loud noise startled her from sleep.

Synz threw the covers off and raced to the window to look out. Across the street she saw the brake lights of a car. The reverse lights came on in the darkness and the car sped off. She grabbed the robe and put it on, then opened the nightstand drawer. The cold steel calmed her heart right away.

Synz slipped into a pair of flip-flops and went through house. She turned on every light to check for anything out of place. Her heart pounded. When she went to look out of the living room window, she finally noticed the trash can along the curb was overturned. Synz breathed a sigh of relief. A squirrel scurried away into the night across the lawn. The furry little suspect made his escape with a scrap of leftover food.

It was too dark to see clearly for any distance past the lawn. Synz had decided she wasn't about to be able to sleep and headed for the lived room to watch television. She closed the blinds and then rubbed her forehead. Synz plopped down on the sofa and grabbed the remote and hit the power. The set sparked on and began to display a rerun of the nightly local news.

A few minutes later, she looked out of the blinds again. The neighborhood was quiet. She lay back on the couch and dozed off fitfully.

The next morning sunlight hit Synz's face through the slices of the blinds and woke her. Her body was sore and tired from the lack of sleep. Synz willed herself to go out and get the paper. As soon as she opened the door, her heart began to beat as if it would come apart. Synz clutched her chest and went back into the house.

She went into the kitchen and pulled out a chair from the table. Synz sat down with her head between her knees while her nerves calmed. She'd begin to believe that she might be on the edge of a psychotic break. She made coffee and added a stiff shot of brandy in it. Something was headed her way. Synz's could feel it in her gut so raw and powerful that it nearly made her sick.

Whatever it was she prayed it would be handled properly. She had an appointment scheduled and called Nicole's House of Magnificence to confirm it. The receptionist answered and told her to come in. She headed out to mid-town.

A black Cadillac whipped up next to her as she rolled in and a woman rushed out of the driver's seat. The service was top-notch and she was barely in the door when she was greeted. The woman from the car was seated with a frustrated air on her face. Synz waited patiently while the receptionist's looked for her reservation. The host smiled shyly and then asked for her name.

Her quest in comfort was on when she got in the chair for a facial. She had scheduled a manicure, pedicure, and a body wrap with a full body rub down with warm rocks. After her facial, the host led her to a massage bay. She opened the door and invited Synz to step inside. The delicate peach walls and scant light gave the room a cozy feel. Soft tune jazz with no words and a cucumber melon scent filled the air.

Another woman came in with a basket of assorted oils and a batch of fresh hand towels. She began to pile the towels into a wall mounted steamer. When she was done she turned to Synz and told her to pick her aromatherapy scented oil.

"Do have you any objections to a male masseuse?" the woman with the basket asked.

"No"

She positioned her face in the hole on the table then closed her eyes and waited. She heard someone else enter the room and assumed it to be the massager.

"Hello" the voice said.

"Hi, I'm stressed and I need this. No offense but if went can skip over the small talk please just do what you do."

"With pleasure."

Warm oil dripped down her back and strong fingers rubbed into her muscles. About fifteen minutes later she felt hands travel closer inside her thighs. The hands knew just how to handle her. They changed in the way they connected with her skin, like an unforgettable lover's caress. The stress began to seep from her like melted butter and her muscles relaxed.

Her thighs parted slightly, while long thick digits worked her past all limits of anything ladylike. The liquor, the music, the uptight day, and the paranoia had weakened her senses. She gave to the bliss and just enjoyed the moment. The experience was magical.

"Turn over" the masseuse urged.

Chapter Twenty - Diamond Based Plan

Soft supple lips kissed on Synz lower thighs in a swirl pattern. Strong hands rolled her and she squirmed her way onto her back. The tongue and the technique solved the mystery as that first touch hit her. At last she lifted her head to get a glimpse at her impromptu lover, just as the first flood of her spasms rolled through her body.

"Damn, like this?" Synz sighed.

She didn't stop and continued to rub down Synz thighs in the. Alex had nearly sapped Synz with little effort. Synz tried to sit up and at first found that she couldn't. Alex came up and sauntered over to with a little pimp in her walk and leaned in to kiss her. She found the strength to rise. A bolt of fury struck when the reality of who it was set in. Synz whacked her twice fast as lighting.

"When I want a woman, I manage that on my own." Synz said.

"Hold on… what is that about? You're slapping people now? What's gotten into you?" Alex asked.

"You've gotten into me. That's how you're playing me. Get out before I make you lose your job."

"Wait, you're okay with giving supposedly that cookie to a man that you didn't know, but you're mad because I'm not a man? I was hoping you were looking for that one would go the distance, that will just sweep off your, little, gracious feet. You're coming off on me hard as stone ma. What you're a boy now? I risked myself and my sanity and this how you're going to play me? Never mind, don't respond to that."

"Risked your self-how? Getting your feelings hurt? Did it ever occur to you to just call me up and ask if we could try again? My biggest problem with you is that you tried to hold both sides of the conversation. Then when I don't react in your favor I'm wrong. I got tired of trying to figure out whether my heart and soul was made of steel or not. I could've changed into a jackrabbit and you'd still be the same person. I changed for me, not you. Where's old girl anyway? Don't you think she'd be the one upset? "

'Baby, that was a little money. You see where I'm at don't you?"

Synz dressed as quickly as she could, and then she raced out the door. The afternoon sun was bright as she drove through traffic on the way home. She replayed the incident in her head before she realized that she had left her panties in the booth. As soon as she pulled into the driveway, Synz burst into tears.

Synz decided that she needed to spend the rest of her day in bed. Her nerves were frayed. Synz made a quick meal of a light salad and a cup of cranberry juice. She resisted the urge to have a glass of wine. Synz locked up her house and went to bed while it was still daylight.

Chapter Twenty One - Hit it up

The next morning Synz woke up refreshed. She made her way to the kitchen to get coffee. When she opened the refrigerator a stench of curdled cream brought her to the conclusion that it was time to go out for fresh milk. Synz slipped on a pair of jeans, a sweatshirt, and dark glasses then left to go get milk from the General Store. Kiyosha rolled up on her scooter just as Synz pulled up at the local store and asked for money. Synz noticed that she had a band on her arm and quizzed her about it.

"Oh that's just something me and my friends got from the mall when we were hanging out." She said.

"What are they for?"

"If I tell you then you have to promise not to tell Mama."

"What are they for?"

"Me and some other girls made an agreement to support one another finishing school. It's not what you're probably thinking. They're just friendship bands."

"What? That sounds close to some trouble in your near future. You better get out and join a reading club or something."

"It's hard in these schools. This ain't the eighties, when it was all free love, wild sex and Boy George. We have lessons from all over the world. Community College is trying to teach us the same material that they learn in the private colleges If mama hadn't of let me come back home; I don't know what I would do. They won't let you pass now if you can't read and write. They make us go to Summer School now for low grades. In a minute they're going to start making us go year round like we're in China or something. We have to stay tight to get through this, Synz. Last year our school had two hundred people the class before us, only one hundred nine of them graduated. Now there's talk about making the Fine Arts mandatory to graduate. We're suffering out here. This is child abuse of the worst kind."

"Girl, the eighties brought crack and drugs wars. You're right this ain't the eighties. Thank goodness for progress. If you make any attempt to quit school, I will put an All-Points Bulletin on your behind personally. Do you understand me? Mama said they used to do horrible stuff to them just to keep people from getting an education. Please finish school."

"I need money."

"You need to finish school.

"Ummm. I meant right now. My weave needs touching up now."

"Y'all new school players are something else."

She shook her head and dug in her purse. Synz passed the money through the window and leaned over to give her a kiss. She wanted to scold her but understood. They grew up in the same place. Success hinged on what your goals were and much you wanted it. However, those low numbers of graduates should've scared anyone.

Some areas were oppressed, depressed, and lived-in a nearly constant recession. Some had so little income that if the economy failed they wouldn't notice. There was something could disturb one's soul about the face of hungry person. There was something equally troublesome about an adult with limited choices.

"Whatever you do, stay in school."

"For real Synz, all we do is stick up for one another. I mean when are we going to be free to get our education without all of this nonsense?"

"Keep your head up and one day none of this will matter."

She pulled off and smiled. Synz wanted give her more hope. Synz just herself begun to gain some knowledge and understood that wisdom came with time. It was Kiyoshi's first year in college. Her cell phone rang as she neared the corner.

"Hello," Synz said.

"Look baby before you hang up on me, please hear me out. I'm so sorry for what I did to you. I saw your name on the list and remembered about how good we were together. Could you please forgive me? "Alex said.

Let me take you to dinner or something, so we can talk. Please don't front on me Synz, because you were with it at the spa, until you knew it was me. You have to know I didn't mean to hurt you like that. Just at least give me a chance to make this right. If we're nothing more than friends, I'd be happy with that. I promise that you're the only woman that ever rubbed my heart the right way.

I'm so lonely most of the time, these little tramps throwing themselves at me when they can look at me and see how I feel about you. I'm willing to work on it if you are. I got upset when you rejected me like my mistakes are beyond the pale. I was hoping we could try again. You came here for a reason. We made love in that room."

"I haven't seen you in years. I went to get a massage. You put your mouth on me in a public place and I'm the one that's wrong. I need to forgive myself first. I'm not sure why though. "

"I shouldn't have said that okay, I agree but the last time I let you think you decided me out of your life. Just say no and hurt me again one more time Synz."

"How am I to trust you when you clowned me? Then when I did step up for you she called you user and a bum, then later I see her running behind you singing that Joe song all off harmony. C'mon who are you playing with? Who told who what they wanted to hear again? I'd figure you'd both be somewhere enjoying my vivid imagination."

"Forget her, I'm here for you now and I always will be."

Chapter Twenty Two - What the ...

Synz hung the phone up. Afterwards, she managed to grab the milk and make it back home. She made a hot breakfast of pancakes before dashed she'd back out to run errands. It had distracted her and allowed her some care free time. By the time she'd finished, it was lunch time. She set out to enjoy a hearty lunch at Karl's.

Traffic had begun to lighten up at one in the afternoon when she opened the door to go in. Synz strolled through glass doors into the lobby and over to the desk. The hostess was on a call and she did a slow scan of the dining room. She'd spotted Dan as he took a leisurely sip of water and read the menu. Her eyes blurred for a moment as her pulse rushed through veins. Synz walked over to the table.

"Why are you following me?" Synz asked.

He looked up from the menu, covered his mouth and yawned.

"Why are you stalking me?" Synz asked.

"Good to see you too Synclaire, please have a seat. You're making a scene." Dan replied.

"I've been making scenes since I was born, now answer my question."

He stood and pulled out a chair for her. She smoothed her skirt and sat down. He reminded her of someone but she couldn't remember who. The man knew where she lived anyway. It was time to turn the tables a bit and find out more about him. The waiter came over to the table and poured water for her.

"Would you like to start out with a drink ma'am," the waiter asked.

"Bring a bottle of Ramirez Coldhearted. She wants the fruit and cheese platter with that. She will have the Spinach salad with Strawberry vinaigrette dressing and no mandarins. A 16 oz. T boned steak, cooked medium rare, with grilled mushrooms and onions. Some Angel hair pasta with the steamed broccoli and carrots mix as well. Add the butter on the veggies, but bring it on the side," Dan answered.

After an awkward moment of silence when she realized that he shouldn't know that.

"What do you want?" She asked.

"I know enough about you to write a book," he said.

Synz didn't reply.

"I was so disappointed in at your reaction to me Synz. I believed on some level no matter what you'd be willing to be my friend. I'm hurt, but you are here now and that's all that matters," he said.

Her brow rose up as she listened. He spoke with confidence, yet something about him reminded her of her younger years. Like a faded rose from a distant past. She reached in her purse and took out a cigarette and lit it.

"I have wanted you for a longtime and when I approached you behaved like you were too good even talk to me. I have tried several times to get your attention. You have brushed past me like I was of no importance. I've enjoyed watching you grow and was hoping maybe you would reconsider and give me a chance to be in your life," he said.

"Do I know you from somewhere?"

"Ms. Welch, after all this time was that what you really wanted to know?"

"Get to the point of all this and answer my question."

"Well, I see you are at least ready to share a meal. I'm a little nervous, because I know you have a short fuse."

"And yet you managed to light it anyway."

"When I bumped into you three years ago you turned me away as a client, but I'm addicted to watching your shows. I've managed to film you on several occasions. So far, you have been very discreet. Your work is top notch. I am a prosperous man that can provide for you. I'd come to propose that you join me for shows that could net you quite a bit of money, with the right business plan that is. Oh, and to be my wife."

Dan had spoken just as casually as if he had ordered a drink. Synz gulped down the wine and wiped her hand across her lips. Her head swiveled around the room and instinctively put she placed her hands on the edge of the table. The large open area suddenly felt smaller than a phone booth to her.

Chapter Twenty Three - Wasn't Me

"What are you talking about?" Synz asked.

Her brain scrambled in an attempt to grasp. He bent over and reached into an attaché' case on the side of him and pulled out a large manila envelope. He passed it across the table to her. She looked inside and saw the glossy pictures. Synz's mouth fell open and she nervously licked her lips and hit the cigarette again.

She flipped through the pictures to find an article stapled to it that read.

Tourist found at Belle Isle Beach.

An unidentified male, 30-40 years old was found by a jogger. Authorities believe the victim was dumped there possibly from a boat. Witnesses reported a dark colored car in the area. The authorities would like to interview the driver as a potential witness. They have been unable to identify the man and have released this composite sketch. The public is asked to call 1-800-WOR-KOUT if you have any information.

There were almost thirty different pictures of someone who resembled her with a guy who looked much like the composite. She got a headache instantly then quiet rage set in. She lifted her eyes up to meet his. The silence that followed deafened her as the wheels churned in her head. She waited for him to say something while she wished she could've stabbed him with a steak knife right there.

The smirk on his face took her back to a murky night. The skin fell from the crack in her soul. Synz began to look for some compassion in his eyes. His smirk turned into a smile which showed off pearly white teeth.

"I must tell you that I am aware of certain details. You saw the pictures. I've tried to negotiate some terms, but I couldn't get your attention without your wrath. The first night I followed you, I spent the night in the bushes.

Such a seductively naughty little thing you are. I've been keeping an eye on you. You don't sleep well most nights by the way. It feels like so long watching you and waiting. I could see the fiery passion in your eyes when you finally experienced a true orgasm.

If you don't meet my conditions then copies would be sent to the authorities. That move might get you in trouble. I don't want to do that. You have until the end of our meal to make a decision."

"Think quickly for what? I'm not surrendering anything. This is about to be longest meal in history."

"Excuse me, can I have the check please."

"What terms damn you?"

Dan settled the bill without further conversation. He took her by the arm and they left the restaurant. He walked over to her car. After he'd opened the door and strapped her in, he then reached inside her purse and clipped her cell phone. He leaned in and looked her over once more with a sneer on his face. She fumbled for her ignition keys. He sprinted around to the passenger side and slid into the passenger's seat before she could find her keys.

"Drive to your house and we can talk there, and no funny moves." He said.

"Ok, but I can be really funny."

She wanted to ram the car into a pole, but that option didn't really make sense with her still in it. She didn't know what he was capable of. Synz drove home and hoped that an opportunity to escape would present itself. She was about to turn into the guard booth lane when he interrupted her.

"Oh no, use the private entrance." Dan said.

"Damn." Synz replied.

She pulled around to the residents' entrance and pushed in her code. The gate slid back and she drove down to her space.

When they arrived Dan jumped out and produced a key. He opened the front door. Suspiciously, he glanced over his shoulder in the shadiest of ways. His eyebrows were knitted tightly together, and his forehead was wrinkled. Her neighbor was outside on the porch.

"Hey Synclaire!" she said.

"Hello"

"I saw Old Boy last night at the club. He wanted to know where you were."

"Oh, did he leave a number or anything?"

"Yes he did. It's in the house give me a minute and I'll bring it over."

His attitude seemed to have changed as he scowled. He waited until her neighbor went inside and ushered in her the door. Dan turned to secure the door before he'd approached her. Synz was clutched her purse and he took it and sat it on the floor.

"I see I'm not the only one that knows a good thing when I see it. Take…take…Take your clothes off," he said.

Thunderstruck she stood there for a moment. She reached out to smack him. He grabbed her wrist and held it tightly. Synz brought her head up to meet his gaze.

"Please take your clothes off."

Her hands trembled with resentment as she began to undo the buttons on her top. As soon as her breasts were uncovered, Dan reached out and touched her nipple. He stepped back from her and unzipped his trousers. Dan had on no underclothes and his massive stiffness sprang out.

The huge dark head fell out and left a wet splat of pre-cum on his slacks. She tried to turn her head away. He walked over and gripped her hair so tightly that her vision became fuzzy. With nimble fingers he reached under her skirt and fondled her soft kitty. Dan removed his finger from between her lips and sucked them.

"Yeah, I bet you're so stingy with it that it's a shame. I just know it's tight."

Chapter Twenty Four - Taste

Dan pulled his moist digits from his lips wet a loud wet smack. He another step towards Synz and ran the same hand along her shoulder the back of her hand. Synz gasped when Dan grabbed gently touched the back of her it backwards. He leaned as if to kiss her, but Synz turned her head away.

The pressure from his hand in her hair had caused her to almost lose her balance. Dan took her hand and put it on his shaft. Synz grabbed it strongly. Her hand had barely managed the width of him. He loosened his grip on her hair and began to pump through her hand. Dan was surprised at the dexterity and the skill of her touch.

"Ahhhh, yes," Dan said.

He began to stroke faster. He massaged her breasts with his free hand. Synz's placed her thumb so the underside of his shaft would rub across it. Several minutes later he grunted, shook him and repacked his tool.

"Let me go." Synz said.

"You have no idea what I've been through to find you. You are uniquely strange, so no. It'll be like having an exotic tiger in the house. Sexy and dangerous, but I honestly didn't think you would ask." Dan said.

"I didn't."

Synz was about to start bawl, when anger prevailed. She had walked right up to him. He was determined enough to try to cage a concrete jungle cat. She gathered her wits. Synz stood up straight and stomped off as Dan trailed behind her.

"You have fifteen minutes to get everything you want to take with you including that fur ball of a dog." Dan said.

She rushed up the stairs and went straight for the Queen Anne nightstand. She snatched the drawer open only to find it empty except for the family Bible. Just as she sank to the floor in disbelief, Dan had appeared in the bedroom door. Synz gritted her teeth. She picked up the lamp and threw it at his head.

"Damn," Synz said.

"You missed." Dan teased.

"Everything has been prepared for you. I have an assortment of clothes picked out for you. If it's not to your liking then order something else. Of course, I removed anything that you might get hurt on. You will be the final piece of my communal, just like I planned. Now let's go and hush up with all that crying. I don't want to see you all swollen."

Her stomach churned with acid. She clutched her stomach right before she vomited all over the floor. The taste of anger mixed with wine disgusted her. Leisurely, she made her way to the bathroom.

There wasn't a way to sure be sure what might have happened when she'd blacked out. She washed her hands and brushed her teeth. Dan was propped up in the doorway and she turned to tell him to leave. Synz spit in the sink and looked over at him as she wiped her mouth.

"Leave."

"Let it go Synclaire, I want you. I'm going to have you every night that I can."

"Is having me worth what it's going to cost you?"

"Is that a threat?"

Synz dried her hands and headed down the stairs. Because she'd traveled often in the past, she'd kept a bag ready to go. She grabbed the overnight bag with her pajamas in it from the hall closet and her purse from floor. As soon as she bent over to pick up the dog. There was a sharp prick of a needle in her side.

She regained consciousness in slightly euphoric bliss. On an extra-large hand crafted bed of absolute luxury. She groggily attempted to move and felt warm, naked bodies under the covers with her on both sides. There was an arm wrapped around her waist delicately. Synz listened carefully and tried to bring her whereabouts in to perspective. She remembered Dan and the needle and shuddered.

"Would you like some coffee?"

Synz looked down into a softly feminine face. She cuddled under her right arm. She untangled herself from around Synz and slipped from under the covers. She rubbed her eyes. A female with long sexy legs, perky beautiful boobs, and a cut little set of buns rolled out from Synz's right side. Her skin was sun kissed bronze and she had muscular toned arms.

"Hi I'm Jenna and I'm here to get you anything you need. That laying to next you is Lacy. She and I will be attending to you. He will be here to visit you in a few hours and you should be ready when he arrives. He might be upset if this doesn't go right." She said.

"Where am I?"

"At home, well this is the guesthouse behind the mansion. I'm sure that you will be moving into the main house shortly."

"Listen sweetie I am not fooled that easily. I'm sure Dan has paid you to act the part, but I'm not kidding. Whatever you saw was just for consenting adult at play. I have a real life to get back to. How do I get out of here?"

"Leave? You can't want to leave Mistress."

"Good morning," Lacy said.

Synz looked at her utter disbelief and cut right into her.

"Let me guess my wish is your command too huh? Well I wish to go back home before Dan comes back and I'm forced to commit a justifiable felony. Can you handle that?"

"Forgive me Mistress, but this is your home now" Jenna said.

"We've been waiting for you." Lacy said.

The absurdity of their words astounded Synz. The indoctrination they'd received from Dan, had given her the best clue about what she might be up against. If these two were any hint of his talent of persuasion. When Synz saw the devout Bianca Tate-like glare in their eyes, she dropped her head.

"Aww shit," she groaned.

Chapter Twenty Five - Take that

Immediately, she imagined Dan somewhere that he could watch.

"I need to pee" Synz said.

Jenna rushed and helped Synz from the bed. Jenna guided her by the hand into a wonderfully decorated bathroom just past a frosted glass etched wall. Synz pulled up her nightshirt and sat on the bowl. The cool ceramic comforted her. Synz noticed as Jenna stared at her.

"Get out," Synz said.

Synz rubbed her temples in resentment. She knew that Dan hadn't managed to this plan alone. Lacy emerged into the doorway view. Synz eyes went straight to her giant pierced breasts. She dribbled urine into the basin. Synz bit her lip. Her eyes followed as Lacy dropped to the floor on all fours. She began to crawl towards Synz with her cheeks tooted high in the air.

Lacy came inwards at the bottom of the throne and shyly started to touch her knees with her nose. She nudged her way between her thighs. Disgusted she pushed her away. Synz washed her hand while Lacy sat on her haunches and patiently waited.

She made her way to the bed. Synz sat on the edge on the bed slowly.

Lacy stayed on the floor. Jenna lit a cigarette and leaned to her lips. She kissed her with the smoke in her mouth. Synz gripped the back of her head. Synz's head dropped down and took Jenna's hard nipple into her mouth. Lacy slid her hand between Jenna's thighs.

Jenna's sparse bush could not contain her large, firm clitoris. Synz sucked her breasts and began to run her hand up and down the woman's slit. Synz pushed Jenna down on the bed and opened her lips and ran her fingers over her tongue. Synz straddled the woman and nibbled on her lips and before she began to grind on top of her.

Lacy leaned over Synz and began to kiss her lips. She wound a moist path down her body all the way to her under her chocolate cheeks. She gasped and Lacy wasted no time to slurp at her rigid nub. Her Cherry nails held her labia stretch so wide her button was exposed and stood at attention. With a flattened tongue she paddled under the hood until she squirmed.

Synz pushed Jenna legs up and ran her tongue in sensuous circles her button. She stopped every few turns; she sucked her firmly into her mouth. Jenna pulled her nipples as she twisted them between her fingers. She dipped two members into her hole and she pulled her securely between her lips. The sexy moans that escaped her lips excited Synz and with a sensual rhythm she stroked her juicy slit. Jenna gripped the sheet and ground her hips in slow circles. After a few moments she exploded.

"Mmmmmm," she whimpered.

Synz stood up and stretched. She made her way to the bathroom to take a bath. It wasn't long before she found herself in a warm bath while the two of them helped.

"Can I help you wash?" Jenna asked.

"Yes you can."

The minute she leaned over the water to grab the soap from the holder; Synz's grabbed the closet tit that swayed and massaged it. She held her position but looked over at Lacy. She lathered up the rag and moved to wash her back. Lacy knelt by the side of the tub to wet her hands and began to rub her shoulders.

"I'm trying to wash her can't you wait?" Jenna said.

Lacy ran her hand down to her breasts at a snail's pace in defiance.

"I can take care of her too," she said.

"He told us to take care of her every need and to be on our best. He will be displeased to hear you how you behaved."

"He clearly said we are both going to be in trouble. He chose Yandi to sleep in his bed last night, not you. You haven't noticed you're losing the little rank you had. The Mistress is going to be his wife, so shut up talking to me."

"I will still beat your ass like I used to. Remember who hurt you until you loved it."

Lacy made it to her feet and walked over and pushed her. The fight broke out and before long Jenna had both of her arms locked with one of hers. She used the other to hold her head under water.

"I'm going to need for you keep my bathwater free from floating bodies while I'm still in it, so let her go." Synz said.

After the bath she went out and sat in a large recliner and watched as they cleaned up. Lacy produced several hand rolled cigars and laid them on a silver platter on the counter and lit one up.

"From now on no one is to see you naked without my consent," Synz said.

Chapter Twenty Six - Shock

"What about Dan?" Lacy asked.

"What about him?" Synz replied.

The women heads swiveled in each other's direction and then over to her. Jenna had just inhaled. The statement made her cough so hard that she gripped the counter amid the attack for support. Lacy opened and closed her mouth several times as if to speak, but couldn't form the words. Jenna paused and stared at her and until she hung her head down and gave up on the idea altogether.

About twenty minutes later keys rattled at door. Dan burst in followed by a tall, exotic Asian woman. She wore an Elephant printed African silk fitted dress and sandals. Her high cheekbones and almond slanted eyes drew attention to her face. She stood behind him meekly with rounded shoulders and clasped her hands together.

"Good morning, my lady has all been well?" He inquired.

"As good as can be, under the circumstances."

"Glad to hear it, let's get down to the business. We will be wed in six days and you will be my only legal wife. The others will remain at your pleasure. I will take you out and show you a around today. You won't be kept captive since you believe yourself to be some sort of entrepreneur or something. I expect you have to give me what I want. You will have to learn a few tricks of the trade. Most of my empire came from the same source as yours. It takes brilliant business sense to build long-term wealth. With you by my side, I might see my goal of being a wealthy man."

"What do you want Daniel?"

"For you to agree to me and not fight, I want you to be with me. I'd trade everything I've had for you to see me as you have seen others before me. Love me with that same scorching passion and look at me with that twinkle in your eyes. Meet me at the top, Synclaire, help me."

For the first time since this ordeal started, Synz began to wonder if Dan was cold and shrewd or just plain delusional. She didn't believe it possible for her to accept his request. Synz squeezed her hands. He waited for her answer.

"I don't want to get married. No hard feelings."

Before she could blink Dan flew into a rage and lunged. He wrapped his hands around her throat.

"Don't you dare patronize me? I have studied you extensively and won't tolerate any bullshit from you. You want my head on a platter or you'd like to drive a stake through my heart. You seem like you would shoot me in the face given half a chance.

You, Synclaire, beautiful and dangerous are nothing like them. Don't pretend with me. I'm still shocked you didn't rip my trunk out of the socket last night. Whatever the astonishment it you'd best work past it.

I sought you for neither a fluff piece nor an actress. I did it because I wanted the best, so don't disappoint me. You are to choreograph them for a show by eight tonight or the postmark on those pictures will have tomorrows' date. I will have it hand delivered to 1300 Bedabs if I have to."

"I've told no you once."

"I'm in charge and you might as well get used to it."

He burst out in laugher. A look of sheer energy displayed on her face. He signaled Jenna and she came to him. He bent her over and unzipped himself and entered her. He slammed into her and caused her behind to jiggle.

"Work it, squeeze me."

His breaths became more ragged, until he closed his eyes and threw his head back. He was into it with full bravado. Jenna moaned. Synz watched him with a raised eyebrow and clasped her hands together.

Dan gripped her shoulders. With a grunt he spent himself and Yandi quickly stepped to the edge of the chair. Dan pulled out of Jenna and zipped himself back up. He straightened his clothes as if nothing happened. He left the room and they stood there in silence.

"I hate him." Yandi said.

"What are you saying? "Lacy asked.

"I'm saying if I did not have to worry about my mother then I'd do him in myself." She said.

"Is anything about this man true?"

"Oh, he's not lying about the money."

Chapter Twenty Seven - Shook

Synz put her hands in her face. Curse word formed a stream in her throat. She took a deep breath and regained her composure. She straightened her back and turned to face her.

"How pray tell would you get away with such an atrocious scheme?" She asked.

Yandi walked toward her seductively. She stood before her opening the robe and graced her eyes with the most sculpted body. She descended into her lap and purred. Yandi wrapped her around delicately around Synz's neck.

"How would you do it?" Synz said.

"I've watched you work. I believe you can pull it off." Yandi cooed.

Yandi ground in her lap as she spoke and it was hard Synz to concentrate. She had a classy air about herself. There was something about her that was internally sexy. The others looked on with pouty faces. The last Synz's wanted was to be in emotional state about her.

"Can I ask you a question?" Jenna inquired.

"Can't you see that I'm trying to think? What is it?"

"I heard that he's made several trips to Detroit to find you, before he bought this place."

Synz rolled her eyes at her. She walked over to nightstand and set the alarm clock to go off in three and a half hours. Synz respond to them by a pat on the bed and they rushed on with giggles. Yandi reached out wrapped her arms around her neck selfishly. Synz rolled on top of Yandi. Synz's slid her hand between her thighs. Jenna cut the lights off and Synz slid on the floor.

For a full twenty five minutes Synz provoked Jenna's body to the brink. Every time Jenna felt the blood pulse in her button like a heartbeat, Synz's changed the flow and teased her while she tried to get relief. She assaulted her with a gifted tongue and sucked her love button like a pacifier. At last Synz stroked her over the cliff of ecstasy.

When it was over, Jenna wrapped her arms around her and drifted off to sleep. Synz kissed the rainbow. The loud buzz of the alarm woke and returned her to her senses. She got up and went to get dressed. She'd just slipped into a short black sequined dress when someone knocked on the door. Lacy answered and told them the car had arrived. Determined to antagonize him, she made her way out fifteen minutes behind his schedule.

She was already out into the night air before the environment came into focus. Synz's took in the sight of the beautiful courtyard. A white limousine awaited curbside at the end of a long cobblestone walkway. She made her way to the car with the young women and said a quick prayer. She raised her head to be sure her ears did not deceive her. She believed she recognized the drivers' voice.

With a blank face on she took her place in the car. She used eyeliner for a pen and took a napkin from the bar inside the limousine. She rode in silence and pretended to touch up her face as the chatter floated among the women. They seemed oblivious and comfortable.

They pulled up a few minutes later to a chic backdoor private entrance complete with a large black awning and plush carpet. She sat back until the driver reached in to help her. She put the folded square into his hand when he touched her hand.

"Old Boy is discreet," she said.

"Yes ma'am. Enjoy your evening women"

The heavy door swung open and the women were welcomed by a large muscle-bound man with a buzz cut and a handlebar mustache. He pointed towards stairs that led up while the music banged loudly.

The metal stairs vibrated as they went up the stairs and through a door at the top. Inside the room was a whole new world lined with tanks full of exotic sea creatures. She found her self-in a humongous private bar high above the crowd of party goers. She turned to peer out of the giant one-way mirror that served as a wall. Below there were patrons packed wall-to-wall that grated and jumped to the music.

Yandi touched her hand. Synz began to center her attention and watched the room. Gradually, the women made their way through the slightly cloudy space. There was an open seat at the bar along the wall. Synz made a beeline to get a Virgin Banana Daiquiri. Dan spotted the women from the far end of the wall and walked up to them

"Synclaire, you look lovely this evening and worth the wait. Please don't keep me waiting again," he said.

He turned slightly and motioned for a waiter. Dan spoke with him in a low tone and escorted her towards a couch where they took a seat. Slow sultry jazz music played through the speaker and created an unusual atmosphere. It was opposite of what played out below the mirrored wall. Dan had managed to create two different worlds under the same roof in stark contrast to each other.

"Your accommodations were suitable?"

She didn't respond.

"Such chilly a mug from such a fine woman, are you displeased with me mistress? Perhaps I could melt some of the ice from your heart, if you would please follow me to the office. We can get down to business."

He produced a key and a door slid open from the wall. The office and theater was completed with seats and a wall mounted projector screen. His office was tastefully decorated with plaques and awards every few feet. The room exuded accomplishment and determination.

Dan walked over to the left wall and slid back yet another panel that revealed elevator doors. He took a key and inserted it into a slot. The doors opened and he stepped inside and held his hand out for her. Reluctantly she entered the elevator. Butterflies tickled the inside of her stomach as the box began to descend to the base.

When the doors open they'd arrived to a lecture theater.

"Make you comfortable" Dan said.

Chapter Twenty Eight -Shake

She walked over to his display wall and noticed several awards on the wall. Synz took a seat that faced the screen and almost instantaneously felt the hair stand on her neck. A female voiced played through the speakers. Her head snapped up and she saw someone on the screen dressed in an outfit similar. The scene was horrific and the face of an unlucky man that was choked with a black silk scarf appeared. The actor straddled his back like a horse. Drool rolled from his lips.

"Turn it off," she said.

"Why, my dear? This is the piece de renaissance and the crème de le crème of all the footage in the world. This clip was responsible for delivering you into my hands; surely you enjoy reviewing your work. This is potential proof that I've seen a unicorn. I'm so disappointed that you were not pleased except for of the frames I printed for you. Every bit of footage is here in this room for my personal viewing pleasure. Soon, I will no longer waste my seed in someone else. During the wee hours of the morning while I gaze at this scene, and wish for you. I have grown tired of watching you on-screen. I will be delivering myself deep inside your womb while your moans play like music in my ears. Six days more and what I sought will be within reach."

"You think so? Seriously"

"You are a mess" he said.

"No, I'm not."

"Well, I do admire the way you're adjusting. Now tonight the stage was set for you. I will perform for a small handpicked audience privately. Consider tonight our first little wedding gifts to each other. If there was anything you would like to do afterwards just let me know. Tomorrow we will meet with my attorneys and get the business end sewn up. That way we can concentrate on our future happiness together. I will catch up with you shortly." He said.

"Well without a bucket doesn't help, now does it? Don't I get to pick what my gift is to you? I was thinking of slipping a flaming pen in your windpipe."

"You wouldn't dare."

"You know Dan; I'm having fantasies of driving a stake through you and going nuts on your corpse to the max."

"You are a bitch."

"What's with the name-calling? That's ugly and unnecessary. Damn."

"What?"

"Nothing"

"You are colder than ice."

"Is that how you feel?"

With his hand in the small of her back he ushered her out of a door. She was surprised to find herself in the basement again. A waiter broke through the crowd and told them the car was ready. Yandi walked and gripped her waist and followed her out the door and into the night air. The driver opened the door and allowed the young women to go first.

"I must say you look stunning. Do you by any chance play roulette? I would love to show you a night out at the grandest casino in town, but I don't get off until nine though. Forgive my hasty approach," he said

"No dear, but thank you," Yandi said.

"It's possible," Synz said.

Everyone turned around and looked at her but said nothing as they made their way to the limousine. The car pulled out into the night and for almost thirty minutes they rode. Finally they pulled up to a secluded mansion on the other side of town. The women went up to the massive wood door. Yandi rang the bell. It was only a few moments before someone opened it.

When the door opened she saw a crystal and iron palace with cages of steel bars. Large beveled glass formed rows of walls that rested on either side of the large hall room. Auditorium style seats surrounded a well-lit stage with several barbarian devices. A medieval stockade and stretcher rack were covered in leather with studs that gleamed, stood on stage.

Along the sidewalls were several sophisticated dark green marble tables spaced every few dozen feet apart. The tables attract much attention. Before she could get to a table, she saw Dan. He had positioned himself directly in front of her.

A server walked up with a tray of assorted drinks. Synz settled on a Cosmo. She allowed him to lead the way as they neared the further end of room. They passed five kings sized poster bed with around lights on them. She was slightly taken back because almost half the patrons were naked. Bodies covered the beds in a full swing orgy.

Chapter Twenty Nine - String

She stopped about a few away from a bed. Dan walked away and disappeared in the crowd. Yandi and Jenna joined her with several other people. A shapely woman yelled out and drew their attention. She rode a man fiercely. A different guy stepped from the crowd and slapped her cheeks as she rocked.

"Get him baby. Look at her, that's some top-notch stuff, right there boy….oh wee" He said.

Finally he unzipped his pants and he removed his trousers to join the scene. He pulled a condom out of his pocket and tore it open with his teeth. He firmly planted himself in her back door. There were bottles of lubricant and condom wrappers all over the floor. Buckets of champagne were placed at the end of every row as the staff hustled about. They watched as they were greeted by a gracious woman with huge breasts in a G-string.

"Hi I'm Addie. I work here. I will show you to your office right this way," she said.

The stench of alcohol oozed from her and she stumbled her way forward. The other women went in a different direction. She reluctantly followed her. She led her down a walkway to a door and opened it. The air went out of her lungs with at the sight of the interior. In the middle of the floor was a pink marbled Jacuzzi surrounded by off-white carpet throughout.

She stepped inside curiously. Synz's discovered the first walk in closet filled with outfits. A second walk-in clear the other side of the room held every whip and toy imaginable. The room had a bright vanity, a queen sized bed and a bathroom.

As Synz looked around she'd accepted that Dan had in fact gone to great lengths for her arrival, which only made her more uneasy. Even though she was peeved, she still couldn't resist a peek at every outfit. She chose a black latex dress with fringes. Synz paired it with black stilettos. A quick check of the vanity drawers led her to some condoms. There was a luxuriant hand crafted whip with suede strips laid on the bed. She took the items and laid them in order. She sat at the vanity to pin her hair up and touch up her face. Addie peeked in to check on her.

"May I have a drink and send down Yandi please." Synz asked.

A few minutes later a knock on the door produced Yandi with a drink. In a chemise she looked like a model for a lingerie spread.

"You asked for me Mistress?" Yandi said.

"Yes." Synz said.

Yandi approached Synz with a seductive sway in her walk. Synz sipped the drink and before she could swallow Yandi's tongue was in her mouth with it. Yandi's delicate fingers went to the zipper and slowly pulled it down. She freed her breast from the fabric and slurped a nipple into her mouth. Greedily, she sucked on it before Yandi dropped to her knees.

The tension had Synz on sexual edge. Synz parted her thighs and ran her hands through Yandi's hair. Synz's guided her mouth to her sweet pot. Her tongue and hot mouth made quick work of Synz's frustration. She leaned against the wall and Synz began to massage her own breasts. She ground out special hot chocolate until it melted in her mouth. As soon as Synz caught her breath, Addie came to the door to let them know it was time to perform.

Synz went to the bathroom and cleaned up quickly and went out. After only a few steps outside the door a soft light stage light came on. Synz made her way out past the crowd and onto the stage. Dan personally introduced her. As soon as she hit the stage, he tried pass over the microphone to her. She walked away and over towards Jenna and Lacy. He motioned for them to drop on all fours with a nod.

They fell in unison and he leashed them and led them to the Rack. She looked towards Yandi, who jumped in to aid. Dan walked over and cued the Disc Jockey for music.

"Never Know Love like This" played through the club. When it came on he leaned over close to her ear.

"Did you try to upstage me? Every seat in here cost five grand to sit in. For that, I give them a show." Dan said.

"You're going to quit talking to me like I'm crazy." Synz replied.

Chapter Thirty - The Shining

With a flirty look, Synz began to assign the young women into position. She signaled for the microphone while Dan stood within a few feet.

"Ladies and Gentlemen, thank you for coming out to celebrate with us tonight. Because of the efforts of my fiancée, we have a show planned tonight. So sit back and enjoy. Again thank you for coming. Somebody dim the lights please. "

Dan seethed when she pulled up a chair to sit in.

She walked over to Lacy in the stockade. A basic wood shape made in a squared C shape, with holes cut out for neck and wrists, and a flip top. Each end had locks to secure the top piece of wood, once a body is inside; it caused the person to be bent over into an L shape while they stood.

Synz attached metal clips with small weights to Lacy's nipples. Her jugs swung. Carefully, Synz added one more at a time until she moaned and rocked in pain. Lacy stood on the Rack bent in half. Gravity continued to expel its force on the weights.

Lacy eyes grew watery. Synz then continued to clamp weights on her pussy lips in the same fashion. Lacy moaned when

Synz slid a vibrator into her hotbox from behind deeply and left it. She walked away to get the microphone and put it to her lips.

The crowd clapped softly as they heard Lacy's erotic whimpers. She put the microphone down and went to work the tool, while she looked over at Dan. His face was the personification of control.

Synz went through various demonstrations of mixes pain with sexual stimulation. He'd conducted his portion of the show as an educational seminar geared toward couples and potential submissive people. When she was done, Synz informed the audience that recordings of the performance would be available to buy after the show.

As Dan talked he looked over and saw Synz wink and blow air kisses to a couple seated in the front row. He frowned and walked over to her. Dan stood behind her chair protectively until she was done. The audience had begun to disperse and walk around the club to mingle with each other and chat.

She waited for patiently. They all walked down a corridor behind the stage that was obscured from view. The crowd ventured into a much smaller version of the main room they began to take their seats. She looked to her left and saw the man and his companion where present. Dan took a seat in a comfy lounger along the wall. Jenna made her way and plopped down in his lap. The man and his lady friend eyes stay glued on them. Synz got up and walked out.

Dan repositioned Jenna to face the crowd and draped open her legs to expose her love nest. The lights went down and the music started play. A few minutes later the soft click-clack of stiletto footsteps broke their attention. The spotlight swerved, just in time to catch a robe covered Synz's as she waltzed on the stage. To his surprise she was accompanied by a total of four people, two male, two female.

The females came onstage first. One went to the left for a chair and the other went and stood by a suspended swing. The males followed with their shafts already erect. Each male went and stood in front of a female. The music started.

The first couple began to oil each other. She was a tall plus sized female and he was a thick beefy man. The female pushed him to his knees. He wasted no time to begin taste her. She grasped his hair and rotated her hips in his face. Synz walked over and lifted her up. She massaged her thighs. The man dropped to his knees.

Dan looked over at Synz and from the scowl on his face, Synz believed he was livid. Dan walked over grasped Synz hand and led her from the stage.

"What do you think you're doing?' Dan asked.

"What you asked me to do?" Synz replied.

Dan grabbed Synz by her arm and led her down the hall to his office. When they arrived at the door he took a key and opened the door. Dan pushed Synz inside of the office and locked the door. Quickly, she raced over to his desk and grabbed the phone. When she'd lifted the cradle to her ear for a dial tone she was surprised to hear silence. Synz searched for the phone line before she realized that cord had been removed. She tried the drawers on his desk as she looked for the cord. Each of them had been locked. At last Synz sat in his chair and sighed.

Chapter Thirty One - Ingrate

There was a knock on the door and Synz made her way to it. Dan waited with his arm extended. She embraced his arm in hers to be led to the car. She was surprised when they rounded the courtyard to a black Lexus with no driver.

"I believed it was best that we spend some time alone. You've a temper and I don't be able to make you smile. I've miscalculated you so let's try to get back on the same page."

She got in the car and hoped he didn't take her for her last ride. She fought hard to remember to keep her temper in check. She still didn't know exactly why he'd chosen her, other than his desire for a wife. It was almost impossible to look at his face so she opted to look out of the window instead.

"You are coming across as ungrateful; after all I have done for you. You don't understand that I have to have you, to care for you, to provide for you, to keep you safe, to make you happy. So far, I have not so much as received a voluntary kiss or kind word from you. Alas, as a new couple we have a few minor issues to work out. Maybe it's the preceding jitters. I promise you, I would be the most generous husband in every way once we are wed. One connoisseur to another, I was hoping you would open enough to share all of this with me, but it appears that I've upset you instead.

We could live a happy and indulgent life Synclaire, please accept me and let's move forward because your hypocrisy is annoying. Spend less time licking on every female that walks in the room. It would serve you best to spend more time being appreciative for me saving you.

I have enough money to move mountains and you will be better-off than you have ever been. You will no longer have to make appointments like a two-bit street hustler. You should be pleased; I'm willing to bring you up from the gutter and that hovel you called home. I'm smitten with the way you think; I wish you'd rethink this. Now, I'd like to stop at the casino for a drink and I expect you to behave. You could be happy but that stubbornness is a problem."

She wondered if perhaps she was supposed to imagine that after he'd stalked, blackmailed, and the attempt to trick her into matrimony gifts. This wasn't exactly what she had hoped for in marriage. He wanted her as a companion. She still didn't know if she had indeed done what Dan claimed. Once inside the casino, she followed Dan's lead to a poker table and stood back and watched him play. Twenty minutes or so had passed when a crowd began to form.

A tall, burly, well-dressed man came up and took a seat and signaled he wanted in with a large stack of Three K chips in front of himself. He looked to Synz and nodded hello. There was something about the way he looked at her as if he recognized her. She couldn't place him. The staff openly catered to this particular patron and from the scowl on Dan's face he was a tad bit jealous.

He leaned towards the man and commented on the diamond covered watched he wore. The man looked back at over at him and shrugged. He continued to focus on the game. Dan motioned for her to move closer to him, a little too insecurely and it showed.

"Hey man that's quite a timepiece you got there. Where did you get that at?"

"My wife. That's a timepiece you have there yourself. Where did you get that?"

He pointed at Synz and she blushed.

"Oh, I just got that. Just picked her up yesterday, we're engaged." Dan said.

"I don't see a ring. I find it hard to believe that she was single." The man replied.

"No, I'm sure she's been single for a few years. Detroit is full of ripe sweet for the plucking."

"You must not be from Detroit. If you plucked her, you'd better put her back"

"Naw, I'm keeping her. We're getting married."

"Is that so?"

The man's pocket chirped and he dug in his pocket to answer his phone. The dealer held the game while he spoke briefly.

"Yes honey, I'll be home shortly. Yes dear, I'm picking up the cream right now." The man said.

The man ended his call and less than a minute went by when a stunning well-coiffed pecan color beauty walked up with a tray of drinks. He ordered a Universal Twist.

"Hello, can I get you anything sir or madam?" The waitress asked.

Dan concentrated on the game and ordered Vodka neat and an Apple Martini.

"Right away sir."

Chapter Thirty Two - Not yours

When she returned with the drinks, Synz reached out for the drinks a little too quickly. They spilled on Dan. He jumped up from the table. The server began to pat at the mess with napkins to clean Dan's slacks. She apologized and went to replace the drinks. He stomped while he'd brushed off his trousers.

Synz was embarrassed that he'd made such a scene, he rammed into an elderly couple and just about knocked the man down. The guy caught him before he fell and helped him straighten his jacket and tie. He sat back down angrily after the older man had fussed over him. The dealer waited until he signaled and resumed the game.

The manager came over and apologized personally and offered to have his garments cleaned. Dan turned his mind back to the game and dismissed the man. The man with the expensive watch was got up to leave. He asked the manager for directions to the cashier.

Synz told Dan that she was ready to leave. Dan had what be a genuine smile on his face. He put her off for a few minutes. She complained of a headache and shortly after they were on their way to valet. Dan reached out for her hand as they waited on the car.

Synz pulled away from and balled her fist up. Instead he wrapped his arm around her shoulders and smiled. To passersby they look much like a couple out on a date. Dan returned her to the room with barely any conversation and locked it. His mood swings had her on edge. He could go from mild to nuts and back in less than sixty seconds.

Once inside the room the women were already there and came over to talk to her. They asked questions one behind the next. She told them she didn't feet well and went to lie down. It gave her a chance for some peace and quiet to think. The women sat around the kitchen counter and talked to leave her undisturbed.

Synz was exhausted and she wanted to go home. She'd thought about how her own actions had brought her to this point. A genuine tear rolled down her face. Synz wiped it away with her hand. Now, that she was no longer the dominate one or in control, she'd decided that she didn't like captivity.

For the first time in her life, Synz could see the tangible plight and horror of slavery. The dreadfulness pain to be disconnected from the only life she'd ever known. She longed to be home in her own bed. Synz yearned for the family that she'd voluntarily left behind.

Synz felt the edges of depression and self-doubt had begun to creep into her mind. She wondered if her parents were worried about her. Synz appreciated that her family hadn't abandoned her; she'd decided to make her mark in a way that she'd known they wouldn't approve of.

Her head hit the pillow and the next she knew it was ten thirty in the morning. Lacy shook her. Synz's sat up and rub her eyes. She stretched her arms.

"You have to wake up. Dan will be here in a few minutes," Lacy said.

She showered and dressed in a crisp pale blue suit and flipped through old magazines while she had coffee and waited. Almost an hour later Dan walked in with three men. He sent the women out of the room and turned to her.

"This meeting will take place on time. This is my legal team. Guys, say hello to my lovely bride to be Ms. Synclaire Welch," he said.

The men spoke and they were seated at the table. The attorney nearest her produced a stack of papers and began their conversation with them.

"My name is Cornelius March; it's a pleasure to meet you. I'm from Johnson, Buff, King, and Hanna. I have drawn up all the documents you will need for name changes, transfer of properties, and added you as a signatory to all accounts with the prenuptial agreement." He said.

"Excuse me did you say prenuptial agreement?" She interrupted.

"It's standard of course, but Yes I did. Is there a problem because that's what I'm here for to make sure we resolve all issues before the happy day.

She stared Dan right in his eyes and spoke clearly and slowly.

"Yes there is a problem. I'm not signing a prenuptial agreement of any sort, end of story, problem solved," she said.

Chapter Thirty Three - March

Dan frowned after he heard and tried to redirect her.

"Well Synclaire the agreement provides for you substantially if there should ever be a divorce and affords me a few basic protections as well. Look at the documents," he told.

"You expect me to negotiate? How could you propose to me the way you did and then spring this crap on me? I guess you have somehow managed to put a price on almost everything somewhere in your contracts."

"Umm excuse me sir. Maybe we should come back at a different time, after the two you have had a chance to discuss this." Mr. March intervened.

He leapt up from the table. Synz accidentally banged her knee under the table when she'd flinched from his sudden actions in the process. The pain brought tears. She limped over towards the bed. Dan rushed behind her just as she made it the bed.

"Synclaire, I need you to sign the papers. Now please get back to the table." Dan said.

Dan was perplexed at the sight of her tears and just stood there. She flung herself across the poster bed. The other men were speechless for a full minute and no one moved. Dan was on blast in front of his attorneys. He had to act fast. He tried to gain control of the situation.

"Synclaire, honey hush up, there is no need for this. Now get up off that bed and let's get these papers signed. I might have to run downtown this afternoon. We can reschedule this, if that's what it takes." Dan said.

She cried profusely and nodded meekly. Her tears hit the covers and one of the men gave her pocket-handkerchief to wipe her face. Dan's brow wrinkled. He seemed confused over her emotional display. He rubbed his forehead. She'd hoped he wouldn't strangle her in front of a trio of witnesses. He left in a huff with his papers and legal helpers in tow.

The women returned with a delicious lunch from Soul Food Connection and the aroma filled the air almost at once. She sat and ate while they chattered. With only five days to go, she had much work to do so and needed to keep her strength up. She asked Jenna to arrange for her to get a dress.

She asked for Wayne Jewelry to have their wedding rings made. She knew exactly what she wanted. Hers and his platinum baguette encrusted bands. Lacy left and returned to the chalet with some catalogs to place orders.

Synz's used instincts helped her through arrangements in a few hours and the basics were handled in short-order. She chose a floor-length gown in Softest Pink with a twenty five foot train. It was strapless with the bodice covered in shiny valentine crystals. She asked a tiara to be made from seven hundred and eighty VS1 pear shaped diamonds.

Satisfied that her choices for the ceremony would bring the elegance she'd desired, Synz decided to leave the plans for the reception until later. With all the glitz and glamour planned to go on at the ritual, the reception had to be calculated thoroughly to match. Worn down from her thoughts, she'd headed to the bathroom to shower.

Synz was still exhausted after the long day before and a hot night of recess fun at last she crawled on the bed and went to sleep. She was awakened in the too early in the day to the sound of a deep male voice.

"Fresh melon, bread and cinnamon oil, poached eggs, and Chiai tea," he said.

Dan towered over the bed fully dressed in leisure suit and looked fresh.

"Good morning dove."

Chapter Thirty Four - Bait

Synz cut her eyes towards him and they'd into narrowed slits.

"Breakfast will be here in a few minutes so get your sexy chocolate moving. Your Jeweler will be here in less than an hour. I must see this headpiece you'll be wearing, it sounds exquisite. It felt good to have the accountant call me to tell me the little woman had run amuck ordering shit. He sounded like he was going to have a heart attack. I don't care but anyway the stones must be paid for in bearer bonds."

She yawned and leaned on the pillow while he talked.

"Synclaire, get up," he said.

Her fist clenched and unclenched while she'd resisted the urge from every bone in her body not to sock him in the face just one good time. The knock on the door broke his tirade. Lacy jumped up to answer and Dan popped her face mouth just as she scooted past him. Her mouth flew open into an oval and she clutched her cheek.

"I'm not your Mistress; recognize a man when you see one."

Lacy looked up from the floor at Synz. She shook her head in disgust. She turned even redder when she felt the tiny cut on her lip. Yandi and Synz helped her up while he answered the door. She dipped in the bathroom and washed off the stench of her late night activities and slipped into a cream satin Brother's robe.

She pinned her hair and quickly applied light made-up and rushed back out. He was already seated. She'd joined him at the table. Yandi immediately filled her cup with tea. She placed her hand on Synz's shoulder and gave it an encouraged squeeze as she poured. Dan noticed.

"I see they have taken a shine to you. "

She pushed a piece of melon in her mouth and ignored him.

"I was sure you could understand their individual talents. I must admit until last night, I was torn between having them back in my bed and watching them in yours."

She smiled and Dan's phone rang.

The Jewelry staff had arrived and Dan told the women to leave the room. He came in with two large armed men with a dainty older black woman completed the entourage. The men shook hands and exchanged pleasantries. Dan politely pulled out a chair for the woman and she was seated. Synz's eyed the woman. She had a briefcase cuffed to her left wrist.

"Hello, I'm Wayne and these are my associates Mrs. Holley and Mr. Chad.

"Nice to meet you let's get down to business shall we?" Dan said.

Mr. Wayne passed her a key and nodded.

She took the key and opened the lock on the briefcase. There was another knock on the door. Both of the guards that had remained upright and stood such in way to be able to reach within their suit jackets in an instant. They all looked up to see Jenna when she'd escorted in Dan's private diamond expert. A man walked and stood behind Dan.

"This is Mr. Thomas. He's here to make sure I'm not buying cubic zirconium of course."

Mr. Wayne relaxed and she reached in the case and brought out a platinum crown stand made in layers. She dipped her hand in once more and produced a yellow cylinder and black velvet cloth. The woman had spread out a cloth on the table before she'd poured out all the stones for inspection. He began to count and inspect each stone for brilliance, cut, and clarity.

Synz asked to be excused and made her way to the women room. Once inside the bathroom, she turned on the hot water in the shower and Jacuzzi. Once inside the bathroom, Synz pulled a single hairpin out of her hair and she laid it on the top of the soap. The mirrors had already begun to cover with steam. She washed her hands and exited quickly and closed the door behind her.

When she returned to the table Mrs. Holley was squirmed.

"I feel like I've drank seventeen gallons of tea, may I use the women room?"

"It's right through that door."

She left the diamonds and the crown on the table and closed the empty case before she bolted for the bathroom. A few minutes later she came out with the briefcase. Synz noticed it was now attached to her right wrist. The men had settled their business and agreed the crown would be delivered to the main house, completed in two days. Ms. Holley turned to Synz and wished her" Congratulations".

Chapter Thirty Five - Wasp

The woman mouthed the words "thank you" and Synz smiled at her, while Dan saw them to the door.

"Wow, what a way to start the morning." Dan said.

Synz began to wonder if the woman had turned off the hot water in the bathroom.

"So now what?" Dan asked.

"You can get out because I have a reception to plan." Synz said.

"Anxious to get back to shopping are you?"

"Something like that."

Synz closed her answer with a kiss on the lips and watched. She made her way to the bathroom and opened the door, just as the water started to flow towards the door. Synz turned off the Jacuzzi before she locked the bathroom door and used towels to dry the floor. She unplugged the tub, got down on all fours and dried the tub.

She searched all around the bathroom until she'd found the small cosmetics case left balanced in the trap under sink. When Synz opened the bag, she pulled up a velvet cloth that revealed a secret compartment with five small lifesaving items. It contained a credit card, a tube of Cherry Bomb lipstick, a single edged razor, an ink pen and a small flashlight. She unscrewed the pen and s found it was loaded with three slim liquid filled syringes. When she pulled out the lipstick, Synz heard a slight rattle.

The container had lipstick in it on top and a pea type dispenser on the bottom. It too was already filled. She heard the women returned and shoved the items into her robe pocket. After she'd put the bathroom to its' normal state, she opened the door and came out. She now knew without a doubt love did exist. No one noticed when she slipped the case into her purse.

The women spent most of the day and helped plan details of the reception. She crafted an elaborate reception. Night fell quickly with her plans nearly done she retired early. Come morning she would put the last touches on the Event. The choreography alone could take at least three hours of practice.

Dan was dressed immaculately in a three piece doubled breasted suit as he walked up swiftly across the lush grass. She tried to muster a smile.

"Bring your ass over here, Synclaire."

She turned in his direction and he was up on her. The wind left from her body as she landed on her back. Dan had tackled her and had a leg on each side of her body. She lay there and tried to suck in air and comprehend. He was near tears.

"Give me my card!"

"That's going to cost you. Get off of me."

"You'd better start talking."

"I didn't know what you were talking about," she said.

"Someone broke into my office and stole that film. A whole wall was damaged. The liquor and a 300-year old oak desk. They even rolled up the carpet."

She wondered if he'd seen the effects of some good old fashioned love. Still on the ground, she found it hard not to smile. She pushed away the picture of his face from her mind. Synz felt bad for him just a little as he straddled her with a look of utter dismay on his face.

"Get off me. I've been here and don't know what you are talking about." She said.

"Sure you don't."

Chapter Thirty Six - Rush

Dan got up and brushed off his clothes and pulled her up off from the ground. He held her arm and walked her across the lawn, up into the mansion. Inside he grabbed her hand took her into an elegantly equipped living room. He began to pace while he wrung his hands.

"Dan, I didn't do this." she said.

Tension filled the room. He stopped and frowned at Synz. She saw light in his eyes. Dan seemed on the verge of collapse with a glassy eyed gaze.

"I think you did it because you don't want to marry me." Dan said.

She sat down on the sofa and the light popped on in her head.

"I should turn you in right now, Synclaire." Dan said.

"With what, some fuzzy pictures and a theory? Wouldn't you have to tell that you stalked and kidnapped me?" Synz asked.

He raised his hand and stepped towards her.

" Look Dan, I had nothing to do with it. I mulled things over. I would have had to have super heroes on my side in order to pull this off and still be here." She said.

Dan began to rapidly pace the floor again and mumbled. With flared nostrils he leaned against the wall and took a deep breath. He rested his head back on the wall and sighed. Dan returned to his normal controlled state.

"That was a three year collection of work in my files."

"You are a nag."

""What did you say?"

Dan went into the hallway and began to make a series of phone calls. Two hours later she found herself in the den, he'd come up with a diamond ring. Synz found herself about to exchange vows with Dan. A man she'd never seen before introduced himself as Dan's friend. The man then mumbled that he was also a judge. The room suddenly seemed smaller than a closet to her and the air was thick. Synz looked out the window and let her mind drift completely away from what was said. Dan nudged her to put the ring on her finger.

"What?" Synz asked.

"Say yes or I do." Dan said.

"I do"

"You may now kiss the bride", the judge said.

Dan kissed her softly on the lips. The judge shook their hands and excused himself, while she sank into a chair nearby. Synz's new husband called for champagne to be delivered to the bedroom. He grabbed her hand and led her up some spiral stairs. Almost giddy like a small boy with a new toy, once inside the room Dan carried her to the bed.

"I want to make love to you." Dan said.

"We're supposed to wait until the honeymoon." Synz said.

He reached out and pulled her to him. Dan kissed her passionately. Synz's stood in place stoically. He nibbled softly at her lips. She sighed and pulled back.

"We are moving way past dislike Dan, stop that." Synz said.

"You are my wife and this marriage needs to be consummated to make it official. The party can still be any day you plan. Right now though, I want to finish the business of making you my wife. " Dan said.

Chapter Thirty Seven - Low

"For the last time I didn't plan anything. Hell, I didn't even realize you were stalking me. I'm tired of paying for something I couldn't have possibly done." Synz said.

"Is that supposed to stop me from wanting you?" Dan asked.

Dan cleared the space between in one step, grabbed her wrist, and then twisted it. Synz screamed out in pain. She tried to squirm away from his grip. Dan shoved her on the bed then began to undress and showed himself to be very much in the mood. Synz rubbed her wrist.

Dan crawled on the bed beside her and flipped her over. Dan had stripped down to his dress socks. Dan pulled her legs up before he pushed up her skirt and parted her thighs to taste her. Synz kicked at him. Dan stood up and reared back his right hand. He slapped Synz with such force that her vision blurred.

"Lay the fuck still, before I strangle you with my bare hands and take what I want just the same." Dan said.

Synz lay there silently. until he climbed on top of her. Dan stroked her hair and began to push into her. Synz stifled a whimper and bit her lip. His massive stiffness plowed into her dry, tight body. Tears rolled down her cheeks.

"Don't just lie there. Do something bitch. Prove to me that you are worth the trouble I've been through. Say something." Dan said.

"You will pay for this." Synz said.

Her words angered Dan and he increased the power of his thrusts. Dan started to sweat profusely and salty sweat burned her eyes as they dripped into her face. Synz tasted the tangy metal tang of her blood in mouth. His weight nearly cut off her air. She threw her legs up around his back and hoped to push him back to breathe.

Dan reached down and hoisted her leg up even farther and drove his massive pole deep inside her wet chocolate womb. His solid thrusts were well timed. He slowed down his pace.

"Yes baby," Dan groaned.

Her actions drew him deeper inside and her body began to involuntarily nurse on him. Finally the leg Dan held began to tremble. He stroked her so firmly their sweaty skin slapped like hands claps. He recoiled only to drive inside her deeply again.

"Let me touch the bottom of that juiciness."

Dan began to hump like an energized bunny. She grabbed his wrist with both her hands. He glided into her with his hand while he continued to hold her leg higher up in the air. Synz was slightly ashamed when her insides became wet in the midst of his brutal assault.

"Oh Synz." Dan said.

Five deep strokes later, Dan exploded while he thrust deep inside her womb. He whimpered when she flexed her vaginal muscles like a vise. Synz didn't want his fluid in her and had hoped to somehow cut off his flow. Dan at last rolled off of Synz.

"Did you like it? That's one of the hottest boxes I ever had. I knew it was going to be good, Synclaire." Dan said.

She lay there and stared at the ceiling. Dan had begun to touch himself as if it were a magical wand. Synz saw his huge manhood was still hard. He stroked it ominously.

Synz turned on her side with her back to Dan. She wanted to bathe. Her body was sore from the rape. She decided to wait for the pain in her belly to lessen.

Dan saw her on her side. Her skirt was torn and a portion of her plump behind was visible. He reached out and pushed her onto her stomach. Synz face was pressed into the pillow and Dan hoisted himself onto her from behind. Dan cackled maniacally as he speared her raw pussy.

Dan continued to dehumanize Synz until the wee hours of the morning. He viciously bit her shoulders and neck in the process. Synz hadn't responded to his attempts to hurt her further.

Dan was so into what his own actions that he hadn't grasped the reason for her compliance. Synz had passed out.

Synz awoke to several loud bangs on the bedroom door. She attempted to get up from the bed in a rush. Synz fell on the floor with a thud. Her body had gone numb. She lay on the carpet expected Dan to come and backhand her. When Synz looked back to the bed, it was empty.

Synz crawled on her arms bit by bit until she closed the distance to the door. With swollen fingers she reached up and twisted the handle. It came open. Synz sat up as the door swung wide.

"I came up earlier to see if you were okay. I was so worried until I heard him say how much he enjoyed what you were doing." Yandi said.

Yandi saw tears and immediately regretted her salty comment. She had tears in her eyes. Synz put her head down. Yandi reached out to for her.

"Don't cry for me, baby please." Synz said.

Yandi looked down at her.

"You're married to him now. How does that work out for me, for us? They told me you're going to send us away. How am I supposed to be here for you if you send us away?" Yandi asked.

Yandi voice cracked when she spoke. She shoved a bag at Synz filled with cosmetics and other items from the cottage. She waited for Synz to answer. She pursed her lips.

"Do you have any faith? Not in me but something bigger than all of us?" Synz asked.

"Yes" Yandi said.

"Good, then didn't stop believing."

"I found that in the cottage. I figured you want to at least have your make-up and stuff, so I brought it to you. Don't worry after a while you'll get used to it."

Chapter Thirty Eight - Crown Heist

Synz managed to gather her wits and make it to the nightstand to hide her case before she went to the shower. She refused to let anyone else see her in that condition. As she showered she heard Dan come in. Quickly she searched his bathroom for something to defend her with. She found nothing. Dan opened the bathroom door and wished her a good morning.

Synz wrapped herself in three towels before she came out. Dan had sat on the side of the bed. She calmly asked Dan to call the Jeweler. Synz asked him to pick up the head piece and have it taken back to his vault, because of the break-in at the club. She explained that didn't make sense to have such a magnificent piece laid out about the house. He agreed and used his cell phone to make the call. Wayne's Jewelry sent two armed guards to pick it up right away.

She'd spent her first night in bed without him. Dan had taken off shortly after he was done with and stayed out the rest of the night. Synz crawled onto the far end of the bed exhausted. He had strolled in and reeked of Scotch and smoke. There was lipstick on his collar.

"Get up. I have moved the reception up to tonight. I know you worked hard on it. I made a few phone calls. You can spend the day preparing for tonight. I had to meet the insurance adjusters at the club. Can you believe they acted as if I had something to with it?" Dan said.

"Really, now why would they suspect you?" Synz asked.

He took off his tie and scowled at her sarcasm then went into the bathroom. She heard the shower come on. Ten minutes later a freshly scrubbed and fully erect Dan emerged. She inhaled deeply and steeled up her spine to attempt to make it through the rest of the day. Synz reflected back on what had happened so far. He seemed to be on top of his game every step of the way.

She sat on up on the side of the bed. Everything happened so fast, it was unreal. She walked over to the mirror, looked at her face and almost punched the mirror at what stared back. Synz went to lie back down, even though she had just got up.

"Look at what I have for you," he drawled.

"Dan, really I don't want to right now. I'm still sore from last night."

The bed shifted and she turned to see what he'd done. When he smacked her across her bare bottom with his colossal open hand, she sat up and screamed in agony. He towered over the bed as she pulled the covers up around her for protection. He pulled at the sheets.

Synz jumped up to run, only to find there was no place to go but behind a recliner chair in the corner. She bolted for it still naked. Her checks were stung terribly. Dan pushed the chair over. Synz curled up in a fetal position on the floor to protect her face.

"Feel better yet?" He asked.

She body shook inside and out. Synz's stood up. His lips moved but she couldn't make out the words. He folded his arms and watched her.

"Feel like you want to be grateful to your husband yet? Get on the bed."

She walked out of the corner and crawled over to the bed. She felt a strange sensation on her back. Synz slide her soft body onto the luxuriously soft mattress. Dan lay on the bed next to her and began to rub her thighs.

Synz's crawled across him and rubbed his chest. She pushed him and rolled Dan on his back. She crawled across him before she took both of his arms and held them high above his head. He reached for her. She smacked his hand and he flinched as she put his hands back into place.

Dan gasped and stiffened his legs when she turned her back to him. When she straddled him then she slowly worked her way down his pole. Synz steadied herself with both hands on his thighs; she pulled up until he was almost out. He reached out and began to grip on her cheeks. Synz stopped and looked over her shoulder and frowned.

Dan's system was full of liquor and it didn't take long before he'd lost control. He grunted as he let out go of a stream of juices. Synz didn't realize that he was about to explode. When at last Dan bit his own lip and spurted thick cream into her womb. Synz felt the hot liquid lava and moved, but it was too late. He'd cum inside of her and shortly afterwards, Dan dozed off.

As soon as Synz saw that Dan was sleep, she reached over to the nightstand drawer and got her cosmetics bag. She quickly grasped the pen and unscrewed it before she removed one of the syringes. Swiftly, Synz uncapped a single syringe and she prayed whatever was in it was acted fast. She moved slowly.

When she spotted a bulge in his deltoid, she planted the needle right into and pushed the plunger all the way down. She jumped back as she expected for him to wake up and swung. He didn't. While she put the emptied syringe back into the pen, she discovered a small slip of paper inside and read it.

"Gacy Pharmaceuticals"

Chapter Thirty Nine - Iced

She waited for another few minutes before she got off the bed. Synz raced around the room and looked for something to bind him with before he woke. She found his cell phone and used it to call the number listed as Cottage. Jenna answered. She asked her to find Yandi and send her to the bedroom immediately with her other bag.

When Yandi arrived she looked confused when Synz's snatched her inside the room. Dan lay on the bed completely immobilized. It appeared he was asleep from a distance. She took the bag from her and shut the door quickly and jumped on the bed. She tied Dan's hands to each other and rolled him over.

When she moved him back over she almost lost her bladder. She discovered Dan was conscious. He was frozen but woke when she decided to put a thong in his mouth too. Dan offered no resistance.

"I can't believe he is allowing you to bind him," Yandi said.

"He's not."

"What. Oh no Mistress what did you do?"

"Just help me put these scarves around his ankles."

"Did he have a stroke or something?"

"Stop asking me questions."

"Now put a mask on his face for me will you?"

She triple checked to made sure he was securely bound.

"Yandi, go and fetch me two men and Addie. I'm going to require all the bodies that are scheduled for the Reception performance. The show has been moved up to tonight. Keep your mouth shut. Go and do what I asked you."

She stood still and Synz could see her tremble in fear. The idea that she might be able to walk away from the life did not seem to register to her. She eased off the bed and went to her and hugged her tightly. Yandi looked at her as if she could not believe her own ears.

"That is still what you want right?"

Her hesitation pissed Synz off. She wanted to hear her say it.

"Yes."

She let her go and was able to breathe for the first time in weeks. Synz's flipped over the recliner and sank down into it, and breathed a sweet sigh of relief. She composed her minds she ran through the past events and sized up the new situation. She saw a box of cigarettes that lay on the floor and picked it up. Synz's found a book of matches, struck one and lit it.

When she turned to face Dan, she inhaled deeply and shook her head at the sight of him. With only his eyes and a small slit for his nose to barely breathe through Mr. Daniel looked quite silly bound and silenced. She propped up on her elbow and leaned close to his ear.

"Well, I am most appreciative of all you have done for me. Tonight, I will show you just how grateful I am. I can see now that you have given me freedom beyond my wildest dreams. And the treasure, oh my, the treasures were far above anything I could have accomplished on my own. I can assure you've made me a much better Mistress. Thank you. I love the mansion too. Because of your superior thinking you have raised me from a two-bit street hustler to an heiress with a private jet. My own club to... wow... Is the how the Monopoly man feels? I must admit the majority of what I have is because of you. So yes I do recognize it." She said.

He stared through the mask; she saw light flash in Dan's eyes.

"I'm going to do what I wish you would've with some of that money. Use it to repair some of the lives you destroyed. Allow me to thank you for all the help you're hard scheming will provide. It should have occurred to you that I wasn't

yours to take like that. I don't really care what your motive was.

You've have no idea what you've gotten yourself in to." Synz said.

Chapter Forty - Clear Path

She rummaged through her bag to find clothes. In a clear plastic bag she found what she had searched for. A long peach sequined gown with a split on the side. The staff stood around and chatted. She touched up her face and in short time, she had managed a classy swept-up do with a few spiral curls. Synz checked herself in the mirror and was pleased with what she saw. She touched up her Heat Red lipstick.

Once outside Synz's told everyone that Dan had a business emergency. She sent the staff on their way to enjoy the party on the boat. Synz decided to step out and speak with them.

"Now just by a show of hands who wants to leave? Don't worry about it, speak up. This will be different around here from now on. If you no longer want this lifestyle then you are free to go. I am admitting on the record that I've no right to keep you against your will. I'm not your maker, so if you want to go your ransom has already been paid. Maybe, there is another life waiting for you." Synz said.

No one answered. It occurred to her that perhaps they had been kept them captive too long or simply didn't want to leave. She feared they had developed an attachment to him. Synz couldn't promise them she would stick around and be their Mistress.

She waited patiently and Addie was the first to raise her hand. Everyone in the car raised their hands except of Yandi and Jenna. Yandi kept her head down to hide her tears from them. Synz told everyone else to go on to the car.

"What's wrong girl? This is what you said you wanted," Synz asked.

"Yes with you." Yandi said.

"Look, if you want this life then stay, but I won't be your Mistress. You don't belong here. You're smart and beautiful. If you'd like to do something else then here is a chance."

"I didn't ever think I would be free, so I what am I supposed to do now?"

"What were you doing before you ended up here?"

"Aiming for a career in Business Management, but that was years ago. I was just getting into it when I ended here."

"Look this life is not a joke. You are so much more than just a beautiful face. If this is what you like, then fine. Find someone who respects you as woman and fulfills your needs. I know you believed that it could be something with us, but honestly sometimes I have to play my part to a get a different end. I have no business at all telling you this, but maybe we ran into each other for a reason. Get your sensitive behind out of here and go follow your dreams.

Go to college, become a ballerina or take up sewing or something. I assure you don't want to try this too long. If you want more than this, then find your will and you'll find your way. Get yourself together before I change my mind. You better not tell anyone I kicked you out of here either. I can't have stuff like this getting out. Something even bigger than Dan, you, or I, is coming to stop all this mess. Trust me this is not where you want to be when that time comes. Tell Jenna to come here please."

Yandi started to sniffle. Synz paused while she recovered. Her mind raced to find the right words to say to get her to understand her position. Synz had developed a protective soft spot for her. It had caused her to care about Yandi, but she had to go.

Yandi finally pulled herself together and slowly walked towards the car. Shortly after Jenna walked over. Synz's looked her up and down and took a deep breath. Jenna smiled at her brightly.

"Tell me why you didn't raise your hand to leave Jenna."

"I want to stay here."

"You don't know anything about me other than what he told you."

"I know enough."

"Not enough to want to spend the rest of your life here."

"Now that you're here it won't be so bad. You're going to make it better right? That's what you came for isn't."

Chapter Forty One - Fo' Fifth

"Yeah, make it better. You better get out and never come back. I'm not keeping any of you as hostages, pets, slaves, or anything. You don't belong here. If you hadn't ended here, what would you have done? After everything you have been through why would you want to stay? I don't care about the kinky sex part, it's what's ever if that what you want. I'm talking about being a prisoner of any kind. He mistreated you. There was no want you want, just what he said. There is nothing noble about being treated like disposable trash. What turns you on in the bedroom is your business. If I let any of you stay you're roles will be different from what you're used to." Synz said.

"I don't care. I think I'm falling for you." Jenna said.

"I like you a lot, you have spunk. The final request I'm asking you as your Mistress is for you to do something we can both be proud of."

"I don't know anything other than this life. I don't have many skills. It's not like I'm young as Yandi. I wasn't that good in school or nothing."

"Ok, but you see how quickly you broke that down for me? You have a gift. It would tickle me pink to see you helping other women. Think about it for a minute. You have experiences you gained from a wild condition. It's possible someone else is going through what you have been through. You're strong and attractive. Take that and do something with it. These little girls idolize everything that comes along. Tell them what you've been through. Tell them how hard it is to live in constant fear and help them find the strengths to help someone with it. You go ahead. I'm going to hang around for a while. I still have some stuff to attend to. Somebody has called me one bitch too many. I have to get back in the house."

Synz watched as the limousine pulled away from the curb. A small part of her died when the car left with Yandi inside. Even though Yandi wasn't her type, she'd grown fond of her just the same. The car disappeared in the night and Synz opened the door and leisurely walked back up the stairs to the bedroom where Dan was.

The shot had begun to wear off. Dan made some guttural noises as he tried to speak. Synz's leaned close to his lips. It took a few tries before she understood him.

"What?" She asked.

"You" Dan mumbled.

"Get out of my way. Nobody messes with my children." A man yelled.

"Didn't I warn you not to bother anything that belongs to me? Where is he....where in hell is he?"

Synz ran out into the hall and froze. Her father was coming up the spiral staircase. She quickly closed the door and rushed to him. He stopped in his tracks and looked at her.

"What the fuck happened to your face." Markus said.

She swallowed as her dad inspected her face. Synz stood still as he checked to see if she'd been hurt. Alex came up the stairs with him and grabbed her arm.

"Where is he Synclaire? I'm going to smash his mouth in, nurse him back to health and smash his mouth in again." Alex said.

"Daddy, he's in the bedroom sleeping right now." Synz said.

"Sleeping, what is he sleep for? Wake his ass up so I can punch him back to sleep. I haven't heard from you in days and when I do hear something it's not what I wanted to hear. Tell him to get out here and face me like a man. He wants something that belongs to me tells him to come get it from me." Markus said.

"Daddy that's not really necessary. I ummm…we got married yesterday."

"Married?" He forced you to marry him. That's all I needed to here. His soul belongs to God but his...."

"Daddy, don't say that. Please just give me a minute to explain."

Synz's father hugged her protectively and walked with her back down the stairs. Markus looked around the house as she talked. When she was done, he sighed and shook his head. Markus put his hand on a forty-five he had tucked in his waist band anyway.

"I don't like this one bit. Let me shoot him the foot at least. It'd make me feel better. A little hot lead is a wonderful wedding gift don't you think." Markus said.

"No daddy. I'm still your daughter. Rest assured I won't stay and be mistreated. If he gets out of hand I will call." Synz said.

Markus hugged her tightly and made her promise there would be formal introductions as soon as possible. She did and stood on her tiptoes to give him as kiss on the cheek. She'd pleaded with him to let her tell her mother. He pulled out his cell phone and dialed January.

"You can tell her right now. That woman is worried sick about you." Markus said.

Markus thrust the phone to Synz ear before she could protest. She gulped and felt her voice waver before she said a word.

"Hello Mama" Synz said.

"Sinclair, is that you?" January asked.

"Yes mama."

"Ask and it shall be given. I prayed that I could just hear my child's voice and know that she was alright. Oh thank you lord. Betty Ann, the girl is on the phone. Where are you? Are you alright?

"Yes mama. I'm alright. I got married yesterday. I've had a long day, but I love you and I'll be by the house soon to talk to you."

"I'll be waiting."

"A box arrived for you at the house. I put it up for you."

"A box. Did it say where it was from?"

"A jewelry store or something like, I didn't open it."

"That's for you mom. You deserve it for putting up with all us. I love you."

"Girl I ain't gonna wear no jewelry. I'll put it up in our secret place for you though. See you when you get here."

January hung up. Synz had imagined her mother shouting and giving praise to the highest as usual. As long as she'd known her mother, January was consistent about her beliefs.

Markus took his phone and put it back in his pocket and hugged Synz again.

"By the way, when I was on my way out the house, this old came and asked for you and gave me this. He said it's you lost it at the casino the other night. I stuck it in my pocket but it looks some kind of credit card or something. Here baby." Markus said.

He reached into his pocket and pulled out the card that opened the wall in the club and gave it to Synz. She looked at the card in awe. She'd been through so much over the card and turned it over repeatedly before she stuck it in her bra. Her dad told her that had to stop and pick up some things for January and head back home.

Chapter Forty Two - Sir Prize

Synz finally noticed a dimmer on the wall and used it to cut down the lights before she went back up the stairs. She hesitated at the bedroom door before she opened it. Dan was still laid out on the bed.

She pulled the sheet back and smiled.

Synz unzipped her dress and let in slide down to the floor. She kept on her thong, bra, and heels as she straddled across his lap. Dan had begun to be able to move but was still securely bound with the scarves. She unzipped the mouth opening, so he could breathe better.

"Untie me right now." He said.

"Yeah, that's not going to happen. Now close your mouth."

"What, you don't tell me what to do. If you don't untie me this….."

Synz zipped up the slot. She looked into his eyes as they grew wide.

Dan lay still as she softly touched him. She slowly scraped her nails across his chest with her one hand while she slid her thong to the side.

The bed started to shake and he began to stiffen his legs. Synz wrapped her hand around his throat tightly and chewed on his ear. Dan blinked several times and then grimaced. His breaths were ragged as he turned on his side.

"Did you just rape me?" he mumbled.

"Maybe"

"Twice?"

"So what if I did?"

"Nothing. I've never been raped before."

"Dan, that doesn't sound right."

"I know, but it's my first time. I don't how to take this. Am I supposed to be mad?"

"Are you"

"Are you going to do it again?"

"Maybe"

"Then I'm not mad."

Synz reached down and grabbed a handful of his testicles. Dan groaned and bucked weakly. He was unable to throw Synz from him. Synz began to twist his sac cruelly.

"Not yet Dan, not yet." Synz said.

Other titles by Inakat you might also enjoy:

Synz Two: Remixed

Sasha N. Deeplee

Smoking Hot Panties

High Maintenance Assets

Coming 2013

Touch of Base

or check back often with the Author online at:

Www.inakat.com

Realechos.com

Inakat Publishing on Facebook

@Inakat1 on Twitter

Synz En Detroit

www.ingramcontent.com/pod-product-compliance
Lightning Source LLC
Chambersburg PA
CBHW070005260626
47159CB00005B/1675